THE MAN FROM FOLLY BRIDGE

JOHN GUTHRIE

Formatting and cover design by Robert Harrison, Seneca Author Services.

For Roger Bacon, Giordano Bruno, and all the other brave thinkers.

CHAPTER ONE

Edie had actually been doing her homework when the strange thing happened.

Well, to be precise, it was the second strange thing. The first one was her doing her homework, in the seclusion of her bedroom. Although not so strange when you knew her brother. Hanny specialised in being annoying. He had the talent for it and the enthusiasm. Edie could work through television, music, arguments, pots being washed, even his background inanities; but not through his determined attempts to cause disruption.

"Edie, you have a pimple. One of those that splat a yellow mess over your face."

"Do you know your eyebrows are going to meet in the middle soon?"

"Does it ever bother you that you're so ugly you'll never marry and will spend the rest of your life alone?"

"Biff."

"*Mum!* Edie hit me, for nothing."

"Edie! Don't hit your brother."

"He was annoying me, deliberately."

"That's no reason to hit him. Or anyone."

So, not so strange that she was upstairs, doing her home-work. Even that was preferable to being in the vicinity of that obnoxious brat.

Well, now that she was here, and doing it, she might as well try to do it well. She could concentrate now. Better make the best of it. With a bit of effort, she might have a couple of days without Mr Meakin's complaints and allusions to her future prospects, which were little better than her brother's. The allu-sions, not the prospects.

She forced her suddenly tired brain to concentrate. But what was it about Maths that always made her drowsy?

When she became aware of a blurry patch beside her, she told herself that it was just a bit of silly dream, and it would disappear when she woke.

It didn't. She blinked, shook her head, rubbed her eyes. One of those was bound to work. But none of them did. The blurry patch remained.

Migraine? She'd had a couple, with reduced vision, vibrating, swirling patterns forming at the edge of each eye. It was prob-ably that, or something similar.

Too much homework. Too much family stress.

It was close, about an arm's length away, if she leaned a bit. And, settling the migraine possibility, it quickly became a sphere of clarity. A bit fuzzy round the edges, perhaps, but everything else was clear, in focus.

She could be sure she was seeing clearly because there was a man looking up at her, as though there was a hole in the floor, and the man was in their kitchen.

But the angle was wrong for that. And the man was not in the kitchen, or any other room in this house.

He was what Edie would have called fairly old, and he wore what looked like the outfit of a monk. He looked surprised, but pleased, and intensely curious. Behind him, on a long work-bench were glass vessels of all shapes and sizes, some of them with coloured contents, bubbling and sending up vapours.

Amongst a variety of emotions, Edie felt a little uncomfortable under the keen scrutiny of the monk man. She felt like the result of an experiment.

She probably was.

Although it was the cliched, traditional response, she stood and walked round the apparition. This provided a view of some tall cupboards and a map on the wall. Walking back round to the 'front', she returned to her seat and waited for the dream to end.

The man's mouth opened and closed. Feeling ridiculous, Edie shrugged, pointed at her ears, and shook her head. The man seemed not to be bothered, but he frowned with thought. He turned and fiddled with something. The sphere faded. The last thing that Edie saw was the expression of annoyance on the man's face.

She stared at the carpet and thought.

What made it more unsettling, even worrying, was that she hadn't had a vision or a view into something mysterious: in a very small way, she and the monk man had *communicated*. She had gestured, and he had responded. If he was *her* vision, then she must be *his*.

She discussed it with herself. This was much too important to have bouncing around in her head.

"Why wasn't that a dream?"

"Because you were awake. Dreams can begin gently, without warning or awareness; but they don't end in the same way. You float into sleep, but you step out of it. And this had no stepping out. And the man saw the end of whatever-it-was. And when the thing disappeared, nothing else changed, not in you, or in the bedroom."

"Okay. What about a vision?"

"Of an old man, dressed as a monk, in a room with a lot of glass jars? That immediately leads to '*Why?*' It's hardly the inspiring stuff of visions."

"Okay, then. What does that leave."

"Madness?"

"Again, pretty mundane-looking for the delusion of a mad person."

"So, what does that leave?"

"Oh. You won't like this one. It leaves a sort of inter-dimensional link."

"To where?"

"Or *to when?*"

"To when. Perhaps through another dimension to the past. Could that happen?"

She laughed at herself. "Oh, come *on*. After what you've just seen, you're asking *could* something happen? Something immense just *did*."

She felt nervous. Not at that moment because of what she'd seen, but because she became aware of the long conversation with herself. That wasn't just talking to herself, using it as a means of setting things out clearly. For a brief time, she had become two people.

Two Edies.

"Hmm," was her next thought. Or non-thought.

Mum's call that dinner was ready was a beautiful call to return to reality. Sweet normality. Real Mum, real Dad, real dinner. Almost real brother.

If only she could send *him* to another dimension.

They'd probably sling him straight back.

CHAPTER TWO

"EDIE!"

Even in the midst of the jostling, noisy crowd, the greeting bounced off the walls, passed through a few empty heads, and hit Edie like a small gale.

She smiled and shook her head. "Why are you always so lively, Nico?"

"What's there *not* to be lively about?" He looked at her with mock scrutiny. "Do I see someone who hasn't done her homework again?"

"I did some of it. Most of it, in fact."

"Well, I *am* surprised. So you just want a bit of help with the end."

"Yes please."

"Shall we retire to our usual private place?"

They had their usual way of going to the private place. They separated and sidled carelessly over towards the back of the library. Familiar with the process, they sat down and with Nico's assistance, Edie completed her homework.

"But study my bits, too," said Nico. "It isn't just about staying out of trouble. You're supposed to be learning."

Lively *and* a potential teacher! A very strange friend. But he was so nice with it all. Edie was very fussy. You had to be nice to have any chance of being her friend. Not that there was a clamouring of eager applicants for that role. Nico was her only friend.

She was tempted to tell him about the odd thing last night, but decided to wait for a possible repeat performance by the monk man. There was no way of describing it that didn't make it sound like a standard dream. Well, a standard dream for someone with a mind like hers.

After a little small talk, they went back, separately, to the mob in the yard. An electronically jangling bell rang, doors were unlocked, and the mob surged forward like an army pouring through the opened gates of a castle.

Approximately seven hours later, they poured out, with less intensity, but more wild display of enthusiasm. As with any moving crowd, it was dangerous to stop, so Edie kept going until she reached the gate, then stepped nimbly aside from the torrent to wait for Nico.

"How did it go?" he asked.

Edie thought about it, then said, "I think Mr Perkins exposed the gap between what I copied from you and what I actually knew."

"That's what I said. The copying is an aid, not a solution."

"You'll make a great teacher."

"What? Being savaged every day by hundreds of little monsters? No, thanks."

"Perhaps, like in Brave New World, they'll give everyone happiness pills."

"Nice in one way, but not for learning. I think you have to be unhappy sometimes if you're going to learn. If you're drugged up, you look at the blue sky and think *That's nice.* If you're not, you think *Why is the sky blue?*"

Next time, thought Edie. Next time, I'll tell him. He'll be able to advise me. He's clever, but sensible with it. His feet are on the ground; mine are so far off the ground that I'm upside down.

As they were about to part, Nico said, "Don't just do homework assignments. Learn in advance. Be interested and you'll *make* things interesting. And don't rely on what people tell you. Work things out for yourself."

More good advice. After they parted, she thought, *I wish you were my brother, instead of that horrible thing at home.*

For the rest of her short journey, she indulged in a pleasant little daydream.

"What are you grinning about?"

Ah, Nico's opposite. The brother. Arriving from the other direction.

Edie retorted, "I was *not* grinning, I was smiling. And whatever I was doing was none of your business."

"Okay. What were you smiling about?"

None of your business."

"Was it the boyfriend?"

"I don't have a boyfriend."

"Yes, you do. Nico. Everyone knows. You're always sneaking around together."

Edie wanted to correct him, but she didn't want to argue. And she didn't want to say that Nico helped her with her homework. Hanny was likely to spread that around the school. On the other hand, she didn't want him to take silence as a confession.

"We don't sneak around. We enjoy each other's company. Now, go and find something interesting to do. Or not interesting, if you prefer. But leave me alone."

"Anything's more interesting than you."

"Then go and do it."

Why? *Why*? Why was she cursed with that thing? Was it some form of punishment? A test perhaps? Survive this and you can survive anything. Plagues, wars, asteroids. She could cope with those. She could take charge of the few survivors and lead them to safety. Although in the case of an asteroid, that would be a very big challenge. Her poor performances in Geography wouldn't stand her in good stead.

By the time she reached her bedroom, she realised that this was the vague and pointless daydreaming that Hanny often caused. Sometimes, the only way to tolerate him was to retreat into fantasy.

After dropping her bag with the thud that always annoyed her mother, and shouting, "Sorry," she stared at the space where the whatever-it-was had been. She even waved her hands about, trying to feel something.

Nothing. No resistance, no change of temperature, no flurrying currents.

Nothing.

Did it happen only when she did her homework? That would be typical of her luck. If this kept happening and became public, they might make her stay in her bedroom for the rest of her life, just to make it keep happening, while people filmed it and photographed it, and found ways of communicating with the monk man. And she would have to keep working, like a poor person in a sweat shop, providing the energy that powered this thing.

"Stop being so silly," she told herself sternly. Obviously, it was just something that she saw in one of those transitional states when you're very tired, hovering so close to sleep that you dream, while never quite taking the final step into unconsciousness.

"Right. Homework." If it made the thing come, fine. If it didn't, also fine, because there was just a chance that her work might be good enough to qualify her for a teacher truce of three quarters of an hour.

Off she went, tapping at keys, writing notes, trying to absorb the knowledge. She remembered what Nico said about being interested to make things interesting.

She tried. She really did try. She worked so hard that she dozed.

Jerking awake, she glanced round. Was that a faint patch, a smear of grey, or was it the effect of tired eyes?

The patch faded, became stronger, faded, then disappeared.

After tea, she did some more homework, this time for the sole purpose of helping the strange man. Perhaps, there was a faint mistiness again, weaker even than the previous one. Then it disappeared.

"That's it for tonight," she announced, just in case someone, somewhere, could hear her. "I need to rest if I'm to be at my best tomorrow." She grinned. "No, not really. I just want to rest. I think I deserve it."

She walked to her door, turned and said, "Don't you?"

CHAPTER THREE

AFTER THREE MORE NIGHTS, WITH NOT EVEN A GLIMPSE OF the fuzziness, she decided that it was in her imagination. "I need a holiday," she said, to herself. She didn't want a school holiday. Or a family holiday. She wanted her own holiday. She was clearly suffering from some sort of strain. She'd clearly been working too hard, even though hard work hadn't brought success. It was probably subconscious anxiety about her lack of success.

But who amongst all the adults that she knew, including the family doctor, was going to believe that? Well, the doctor might, if it gave him an opportunity to shove some pills at her. Anxiety? Try these.

Soma, it was called in Brave New World. Worried, angry, anxious, depressed? Pop in a soma pill and you'll instantly feel happy and relaxed. So terrible, but sometimes so appealing.

"Because, after all," she said to the space, "I *am* anxious about not doing well, even though I don't do much to improve things."

She sighed.

The fuzzy patch appeared.

Soon, as she almost trembled with excitement, the sphere appeared, too.

All seemed to be exactly as before. The monk man, the workbench, the glasses and tubes, the bubbling liquids. But this time, the man looked pleased. He inhaled deeply and held his arms out, palms upwards, as though inviting Edie to share in his moment of success.

If the first time had been an accident, then he had worked out what he had done, and repeated. He was in control.

It was only then that it fully penetrated her that *he* was seeing *her*, just as much as *she* was seeing *him*. But what could he see? Was he really 'down there', wherever 'down there' was? She moved on her chair, and half-turned, to give him a better view of her bedroom.

He nodded approvingly, then looked puzzled as he saw bits of her room. Self-consciously, she winced as she became aware of the mess. Time to change the subject, as it were. She pointed at herself, then tore a piece of paper out of her notebook and wrote 'Edie' on it. She turned it round and held it for the man to see. He read the name, looked at her, then back at the name. She held up her hands and wrote 'Edith'.

He gently waved his forefinger and smiled. Definitely a name. "Probably popular in your time," Edie muttered.

The man had turned and was fumbling about amongst a muddle of stiff papers, presumably parchments. Finding a satisfactory one, he wrote on it and held it up for Edie to see.

Frater Rogerus

Edie smiled and nodded, hiding her confusion. It looked as though it might be Latin. Was the man Italian? Or someone so far back that it was his language? Didn't a lot of people speak Latin long ago?

These were quick thoughts, occupying about a second. The more important thing was to display good manners. She gave a little bow and did something weirdly inventive with her hands as a sort of through-the-ages gesture of respect, for use with monk men, royalty and aliens. I sit in peace.

The man turned and gestured with a look of pride towards his workbench. Then he pointed at Edie and made a gesture to indicate his lack of understanding. It pleased her to compare his discovery with her long, rambling equations, which went in clear, logical progression to a completely wrong answer.

But what next? They had exchanged names, sort of, and she understood that he was a scientist. But apart from the name, she didn't know who he was, or, returning to the constant problem, *when* he was.

It was time to call in the troops, in the form of her more learned friend.

Not knowing what to do, she smiled at the man. He smiled back, in a distracted way, as though there were more important things to do than smile at each other. She couldn't disagree.

He opened his mouth to speak, then closed it and frowned darkly. He turned to his right and spoke sharply. Next, he looked round in haste, disappeared to Edie's right, then appeared briefly with a crate, which he put in front of Edie, almost blocking her view.

She saw him walk to her left, then return, followed by another man. Her view of him was very restricted and brief, but she had the impression of a tall, thin man with sharp features. Both men disappeared for a little while. Suddenly, the crate was pulled away, and the visitor was looking at her, his face twisted with rage and contempt. Much of it seemed to be for her, as though she had been personally involved in the experiment.

The tall man turned and shouted at the other man. Turning back, he disappeared under the sphere. Edie looked at the monk man. He waved her back urgently.

She soon found out why.

Almost filling the sphere was the thin man's face.

It started to come through, pushing through something like a clear, jellyish substance.

And worse. With a tearing sound, he reached through and grabbed her arm, and started to pull.

Terrified, Trying to keep away from the sphere, Edie jabbed hard at his nose. He yelped and toppled, falling back out of sight. Beyond him, the other man broke some glass phials, and the sphere disappeared. It faded into the blur, then vanished.

Edie sat back and exhaled, still shocked, trying hard to think about what had happened.

Looking through the sphere, being looked at through the sphere, by someone who clearly didn't mean her any harm, was interesting and exciting.

Being grabbed by an angry man who came through the sphere, and tried to pull her through it, was horrifying. The thought that he could reach through and touch her! She had an enemy, who could climb through into her time, and could do whatever he wanted.

She had no doubt that what he wanted was to harm her.

It was definitely time to call in the troops.

CHAPTER FOUR

NICO LOOKED AT HER AND TILTED HIS HEAD, LIKE AN inquisitive animal.

"You don't believe me," Edie said.

"No, no. Well, yes. I mean, I do believe you. It's just that I wonder whether ... well, in the heat of all the excitement, some of it might have become a bit distorted."

They were sitting under the big oak tree which stood in a sort of neutral territory in the middle of the big field. All around them, various lunchtime games were being played, or not played. At any moment, they might be interrupted, but most people were making the most of the time away from lessons.

Edie looked away, but not really seeing the shouting, running students.

"No," she said. "Nothing was distorted. It all happened exactly as I said. I know that it's weird, and a lot for you to take in, all in one go, but it's happened twice, and it was all exactly as I said."

"Okay, then. Have you looked up any of this?"

"No. I came to you first."

"Well, I'm flattered. But as with all mysteries, the first step is the internet. On the grounds that this is important research, I shall have a quick look."

He switched on his mobile telephone, tapped in his question and very soon exclaimed, "Ha!"

He held the screen out for Edie to see at the same time.

"Roger Bacon," he read, selectively. "1220 to 1292. Scientist, philosopher, mathematician, Franciscan monk. Hmm. It all fits. And it's hardly the sort of stuff that you'd know about. No offence."

"None taken."

"And he was here, in Oxford. He lived on the Folly Bridge."

That rang a bell. It was one of those mandatory items in guide books. The great scientist and philosopher who lived on Folly Bridge. But it had never lodged firmly in her mind. And, so far, he hadn't been in any of her lessons. She couldn't even recall that century being mentioned.

Nico hesitated before speaking again. "Look, Edie, you know that I have absolute trust in you. But there are two things here. One is that most people have absolute trust in scientists, doctors, religious leaders, politicians; and much of the time, they're wrong. It's a matter of principle. The second is that, well, so far, it's *your* experience. I want to share it . I want it to be *my* experience, too. And then it would be *our* experience. Understand?"

"Yes. Of course I do. I want you to see it, too. Then, I'll be able to stop explaining it all to you, trying to convince you; and you can stop believing me because we're friends. You wouldn't need to believe me. You'd see it for yourself. And we can work out a plan, strategy, that sort of thing. And, most important, when it comes to pushing a nasty man away, two are better than one."

"Good point."

"The problem is that I don't know when, if ever, it will appear again. That Mr Bacon looked surprised when he first saw me. He was probably working on something very different, and I was just a … by product?"

"Very likely. And to keep that bad man away, he might have destroyed the only means of producing it. He might not know what amount of this and what amount of that actually did the trick."

"And there might be strict surveillance. He might even be put in prison, or killed. That's the sort of thing they used to do to scientists."

"We can make some sort of progress with that."

"How?"

"We can read about him. For example, if he died naturally, he wasn't executed."

"He could have been poisoned."

"Well, true. But look at it this way. If his experiments with this whatever-it-is, was, were known and recorded, I think that it would be a pretty significant bit of history, wouldn't it? We'd all know about it. So, either he didn't try again, or he did it all in secrecy, or the records were destroyed."

"So we might be involved in an important bit of history which never became history?"

"Yes, I suppose it could be."

"I want him to do it again, but I don't want that horrible man reaching in and grabbing me."

"That coming through is probably the weirdest part. A seeing link to the past is pretty big, but someone reaching through from the past and grabbing you is, well, fantastic. And frightening, of course."

"Especially when he might be able to come all the way through."

"Sit back a bit to avoid the grabbing, and have a weapon of

some sort. And don't be afraid to use it. We don't know what he might do to you."

Edie sighed. "It probably won't happen again. Mr Bacon would be under the threat of something horrible. His exciting experiment would be seen as devil's work, anti-God, all that sort of thing. He probably never tried again."

"Or couldn't because he didn't know what he'd done."

"How frustrating for him. Knowing that he'd done a tremendous thing, but not knowing exactly what he'd done or how to do it again."

"And being in danger for doing it it, with his enemies breathing down his neck, watching for any deviations from what they considered to be the right way. The usual thing. Do all the research you want so long as it doesn't interfere with the pursuit of ignorance."

"I'm going to read about him tonight, and look for any clues."

"Please, Edie, homework first. Possible trouble in the past is one lurking problem; try to avoid trouble in the present, too.

Edie nodded. That was good advice.

She needed plenty of that.

CHAPTER FIVE

"You're just making use of me," Nico said.

Edie knew he was teasing. But some homework help was very welcome.

While they waited, and hoped.

There was also the substantial excuse of the class project on which they were working together.

First, homework," said Nico. "Try to do it on your own, while I do mine. Yes, I'll look at yours and give you some hints. That doesn't mean doing it for you. Then, we'll have a go at the project. And hope that something happens."

"Right. And perhaps a little more to the right. It might not happen in exactly the same place." She had a sudden alarming thought. "A bit more. I'll move round, too. It might not be a good thing if the link happened right where you're sitting. You might be in both times at the same time, if you see what I mean."

Nico nodded and looked nervous as he shuffled his chair closer to hers.

A week had passed since the last occurrence. In that time,

they had waited for the opportunity that the beginning of the project provided. Now, no-one could complain about their working together in their own time. Edie's bedroom didn't have full parental approval as the best place for doing their work, but with frequent checks through such feeble excuses as the possible need for drinks, and a lot of well-established trust, there was no interference.

After a week, there was no strong reason for it to happen this evening, but Edie 'had a feeling'. And with her potential witness beside her, she was almost willing it to happen.

Nico plunged into his homework, and with a raised eyebrow suggested that she do the same. Edie didn't quite plunge. She walked slowly into the cold depths of the work.

So slowly that she was still making her way from the shore when it happened.

It was very brief. It barely moved from the blurry stage. There was just a short glimpse of the face and arm of Mr Bacon as he threw something. Then the view faded and disappeared.

"You saw that, didn't you?" Edie spoke very quietly. Knowing that he must have seen it increased the drama.

"Yes," Nico answered. "I saw it." He bent down and picked up the thing which had been thrown.

A small book, with a red leather cover, and thick pages of writing inside.

"Latin, I think, most of it," Nico said. "Some in other languages. Some in signs, symbols, perhaps. A lot of pictures. And, as you'd expect, a lot of equations. And other sums."

"His experiment," Edie said firmly. "Either that other man wants to destroy it, or he wants to make use of it. Mr Bacon has sent it to us for safe keeping."

Nico pondered. Edie read his thoughts. "Which means that we must hope the nasty man doesn't find a way of coming to look for it."

"If he needs the book to do it, then the only way would be to gatecrash one of Mr Bacon's sessions, or …"

"…force him to make the link and keep him restrained until the nasty man has come through."

She leaned back in her chair and said, "I'll be honest with you. I'm frightened."

"I'd better stay as close as I can, as much as I can."

"Yes."

While he was talking, Nico was flicking through the pages, glancing at words, hoping to understand some. He said, "Ah. On the inside cover. A message, I think."

"What does it say?"

"Latin, I think. Cave Vadigan. I think 'cave' means beware."

"And Vadigan is the nasty man?"

"But how are we to beware of him? A few instructions would have been helpful."

"He probably doesn't know. This Vadigan certainly disrupted him and made him afraid."

"He's probably someone with a lot of official power, a senior churchman, who disapproves of Mr Bacon's experiments."

"Just what I need. Someone from hundreds of years ago who doesn't like me. As though I don't have enough problems."

"Poor Edie. But remember that you have one great weapon against your enemies."

"What's that?"

"Me."

* * *

"In the meantime," Nico said. "Let's turn from that and do …."

"Oh, whaaat? Really? With all this excitement?"

"The excitement might come later. Nothing is happening

just now. Let's clear some of this school stuff, and have more time for whatever might come later."

"You are annoyingly sensible."

He grinned. "Just what you need."

"Yes, okay. Let's do it."

An hour and twenty minutes later, the homework was done, and a start had been made on the project.

"Time to go," said Nico.

"Must you?"

"Yes," Nico replied with emphasis. "But, up to a reasonable time, keep in touch in the usual way." He held his mobile telephone up and smiled. "You won't be completely alone."

"No. I might have this Vadigan man with me."

They shared a half-hearted laugh. Nico went home, and Edie did her best to have a reassuringly ordinary evening. She didn't bite at any of Hanny's dangled baits, especially his silly innuendoes about what she and Nico had been doing. Edie had an ally in her parents, who immediately stepped on his silliness. Subdued, he settled for muttering about whatever the family were watching. Edie didn't mind that it was dull. She had decided that dullness had a strong appeal when the alternative was danger.

When it was time for bed, the short walk upstairs made her feel like a frightened little girl again. She felt the looming oppression of loneliness.

In bed, she looked at some pages of the book, but didn't understand any of it, gave up and put it under her pillow. She had a pleasant chat with Nico, then settled down to sleep. And she soon slept, deeply and calmly.

She woke, somewhere in that deep and lonely darkness of the very early hours, when the early morning is still attached by black strands to departing midnight.

She knew instantly what had wakened her because she saw the pale glow of the sphere.

She lay still, incapable of deciding whether to go and look, perhaps into the friendly face of Mr Bacon, or …..

There was a whoosh, a brief tearing, and something blacker than the night darkness hurtled out of the glow and landed in a heap on the bedroom floor. The heap quivered, writhed and rose into the shape of a tall man.

Vadigan had come.

The sphere winked out.

He looked quickly round, saw her and walked quickly towards her bed, hissing, "Where is it?"

Edie yelled, louder than she had ever done before. It was piercing and jarring. The instant response was the opening of a bedroom door and feet hurrying along the landing.

This time, he hissed with rage, turned and strode away to the window. He opened it, and with only a brief glance, leapt out.

She heard him land as her father flung open her door.

CHAPTER SIX

"At first, I think Dad was annoyed when I said I'd had a bad dream. I think he wanted something more interesting to be happening."

"Which it was."

"But when the stress had its effect and I started crying, he and Mum took turns to comfort me."

"A *lot* of stress. It must have been horrible."

"Not just coming through, but the way that he did it. He must have arranged things on the other side to have a run at the sphere, to have the power to come through that barrier stuff in one leap. He came through and hit the floor like a great, shapeless bat. Then, he unravelled and rose to his great height. Well, it looked like a great height to me, terrified in my bed."

Nico nodded, but didn't speak. He was worried for his friend, but didn't want it to show. His job was to sympathise, but to try to lead her away from anxiety. He smiled and said, "If the sphere appears again, you could throw the book back."

"And he'd run after it, like a dog after a ball."

They both laughed at the thought, which is what Nico had

intended. He added, "At least he knows now that your parents are close and quick to respond."

"True. But I'm sure he'll keep trying. That's why it's in my bag. We're all out during the day, and he looks like the sort who could open a door easily."

"Yes, that makes sense. Just don't lose your bag."

"I know. That's another worry. We do so much lugging about from lesson to lesson. Tomorrow, it's swimming. Coach, changing rooms, everything in a scramble."

"Just keep saying to yourself, every time you move, *Bag, bag, bag.*"

"Yes, yes, yes. But you know me."

"Well, I know that you're usually thinking several things at once. That's fine. Just have this check in place, every time that you go anywhere."

She gave him a thumbs-up, but said, "It would be funny, or very dangerous, if he did corner me somewhere, and I had to say to him that I'd lost it. He'd be very upset."

"Yes. That raises another point. If it's 'the book or your life', you'll have to admit defeat and give him the book."

"Hmm. In that case, perhaps I need to hide it somewhere."

"At my place?"

"Possibly. Although he might find out about you. He might take a few days now to adjust and adapt."

"Yes. That's a good point. And here's another. I've often thought about time travel, and one thing occurred to me. If you move centuries forward or backward, you're going to encounter germs which don't exist yet or don't exist anymore. I mean, germs to which we've become immune, or haven't, if you see what I mean. He is now in the midst of germs which didn't exist in his time, or to which he hasn't become immune, as we have."

"Like War of the Worlds?"

"Yes. At the least, I suspect that he is currently suffering from a very bad cold."

* * *

FOUR DAYS WITHOUT ANY SIGN OF VADIGAN suggested that Nico was right. "Or," he added, "or and ...."

"Do you mean 'and stroke or'?"

"That's right. But the other other way round, although I suppose it's more or less the same thing."

Edie nodded to encourage him. "Oh, right," he said. "It's the old thing of thinking as your enemy is probably doing. This man has arrived here, in a big rush from the 13th century. Now, when he came hurtling through the sphere, did you notice a suitcase? Exactly. He hasn't stopped to plan all this, which immediately shows a weakness. But more importantly, at this stage, it means that in addition to the germs, he has no suitable clothing, and, in view of the fact that most towns for miles around didn't exist in his day, or were tiny villages, he probably has no idea where anything is."

"So, he's like a large purple alien. He needs to be inconspicuous, while trying to blend in."

"That's right. He needs clothes. He needs money. He needs money for clothes, unless he steals them."

"But you're assuming that he's going to be here for a while. He might be intending a quick snatch and return."

"No sign of that so far. At least, not since the first attempt."

"He might be lurking in a dark place, waiting for the right moment."

"Edie, this is twenty first century Oxford. There aren't dark places for thirteenth century villains to lurk."

"Plenty of trees along the river."

"Well, he can stay there as long as he likes. He wouldn't

accomplish anything. No. My guess is that he will find some clothes and disguise himself."

"I'd recognise him."

"Right. *You* would. What would you do about it? Report him to the police? Tell your parents? He probably wouldn't care that you did know."

"I think you've forgotten your reassurance role."

"Oh. Sorry. I was just thinking of possibilities. Very likely, he's not doing any of those things. Perhaps he's given up and gone home."

"How?"

"The same way that he …hmm, that's an interesting one. If the sphere isn't there, perhaps turned off, so to speak, by Mr Bacon, how is Vadigan to return, with or without the book?"

At that point, the bell rang. Still pondering, they went with the crowd into the school.

Just before they parted, Nico whispered excitedly, "Perhaps he'd use the book to make his own link."

CHAPTER SEVEN

FOR TWELVE DAYS, HE BARELY MOVED. HE LAY IN THE darkness of his hiding place, and suffered. The chest cold was just the beginning. The thankfully short journey to this temporary home had been a wading through a thick mist of unknown, invisible things that wanted to kill him. He didn't understand the details and didn't want to, but he knew that in another time, as in another country, diseases and their causes would be different.

Then came a succession of ironies. In this time, there would be medicines to overcome the ailments in this time, but his ailments, his responses, would be new ones, and his body would be an old one. He couldn't even begin to solve the problem because he couldn't even focus on it. It was like trying to catch an insect which just kept turning in another direction. Everything: illness, medicine, himself, seemed to be simultaneously here and there and useless.

He couldn't build a return sphere until he had the book, but even if he went back, he would have modern diseases, for which old cures might not work. He might even be the beginning of a plague.

He might have done that here.

He had not prepared for any of this. The plan had been to enter the room, grab the book and return before Bacon released himself. He should have realised that all Bacon had to do was twist round, thrust out a leg and break a phial of connecting fluid. As soon as he saw the disappearing sphere, Vadigan knew he was in trouble.

At night, he crawled out for any bits of food and water that he could find, even though he knew he was consuming yet more dangerous things. But there were herbs. He knew about herbs. Although he was in a large town, with most ground covered by concrete, herbs persisted, as they had always done. He wasn't sentimental, but it softened his hardness to see the old plants persevering in spite of all the horrors that had led to this new world.

But there was a horror almost as bad as the illnesses consuming his body. As soon as he staggered out of the garden of that annoying girl, there was a hideous roaring, and blinding lights, and something rushed past him. A dragon on wheels. It was soon followed by another one. He lurched along, keeping close to garden walls. Looking through a gap in the houses, he could see more in the distance, going right and left, their eyes blazing, and their mouths roaring.

He became aware that he was panting. Immediate illness, and terror from these fiends from hell. What else could these dazzling, roaring, hurtling things be? They must now be in control of humanity. As it was prophesied, roughly speaking.

He was still working his way through the various, possibly applicable, Biblical references when he saw simultaneously what appeared to be a dead dragon ahead, two doors being opened, and two people squirming on each side. There was a muted roar, lights appeared, and the dragon rolled away.

But not a dragon, he admitted; clearly, some form of fantastically controlled, horseless, waggon.

He was becoming weak when he saw a small wilderness of rocks, brambles, long grass and nettles, sloping away from the road to a stream. Comfort was not a priority, or even a concern. He barely felt the stings and scratches as he scrambled and slithered into the welcome seclusion.

As soon as he stopped moving, he sank into a sleep of utter exhaustion.

* * *

He woke to the torments of his steadily increasing illnesses. It was as though he had been given a metaphorical bag of diseases on entry into this time. He sweated, shivered, had violent headaches, pains in his limbs and insides.

His first brief forays after dusk provided dandelions, nettles, willowherb, mugwort and plantain. He had no means of cooking any of it, which made the nettles difficult, but he squeezed until the poison was in his fingers, and ate the neutralised leaves. Besides, he reassured himself as he tried to ignore the stinging in his fingers, he was trying to fight whatever was harming him, so perhaps some nettle poison would be beneficial. He ate various leaves, some of which which were not good or safe eating, but his purpose was less to provide nutrition, more to remove poisons from his body.

He was a man of strong will. He resisted the slight temptations of dustbins, knowing that unfamiliar food, already discarded by the local people, was not likely to be good for his own body. He could wait.

Provided that he didn't die.

As the days, the cold nights, passed, he shivered and sweated, and coughed and gasped. Sometimes, he curled up and groaned. Sometimes, it was tempting to give in and die there, anonymous, all the secrets safe. Except that they wouldn't be. That infuriating girl still possessed what must be the most important document ever to fly through the centuries.

He *must* take it back and destroy it.

Bacon's scientific experiments were the work of the devil. Especially this one.

And that meant using the book of evil, or what Bacon made with it, to permit his own return.

Well, means to an end. He must do whatever was necessary. He must use evil to destroy evil. He wouldn't be the first great man of religion to have that dilemma. Far from it.

Find the book.

Take the book.

Use the book.

Destroy the book.

He *must*.

He *would*.

And in order to do all that, he had to survive.

* * *

HE BECAME AWARE OF VOICES, DRIFTING DOWN LIKE particles of dust into his dark place. Children's voices. As well as he could in his feeble state, he made his body tense, ready for escape, even though he had nowhere to go. But the voices didn't come nearer. At first, he thought they were, but he soon realised that they were merely louder, as excitement or arguments burst out.

The children were playing, arguing, laughing in the long grass, and sometimes in the brambles. In the days that followed, they often came, always playing the same exuberant games, which Vadigan soon realised were play-fighting. And they had strange quiet conversations into small things which they held to their ears.

Seeing possible danger converted into possible opportunity, he crawled a little way up the slope until he was much closer. Then, he listened.

He listened for days, patiently translating the incomprehensible foreign language of present form and present slang into something vaguely comprehensible. Each night, in the enfolding silence, he wrote out mental pages of notes of what he had heard, dissecting and analysing. He soon realised the Latin origin of many words, the Saxon and Norse origin of others. Bit by bit, root and stem, he managed to build his understanding of this new language.

He knew that this was his most powerful weapon, his most powerful tool.

Yes, he needed clothes, and money, and things to make him well again.

But now, he could walk amongst people and ask for things.

Each day, before the children came, he moved a little closer, crawling up the slope, and making a second home in the middle of a bramble bush, which he was pleased to find still had a few blackberries. Then, he lay still and listened. Progress was very slow. It wasn't just the words: there was the way that they were spoken, in a rapid gabble of partial words, panted or rattled out, until, eventually, the common phrase, in the common inflection: "I'm bored."

One day, there was only one voice, a solitary muttering, in time to the crunching and scuffling of a solitary pair of feet. Peeping out, Vadigan saw a small boy, playing an imaginary game, thrusting and parrying with an imaginary sword.

This was, must be, the moment.

"Boy!" His voice was weaker then he expected, but that suited his purpose.

The boy stopped with a nervous jerk, and peered into the gloom, ready to run away.

"Fear not," called Vadigan. "Old man, need help. Please help."

The boy advanced cautiously and looked at the figure amongst the thorns. "You a tramp?" he asked.

Vadigan took a chance and said, "Yes."

The boy tutted."There's a lot of poor people now. We didn't have a holiday this year, apart from a few days down at Sandy Bay. Not much fun is it, being poor?"

"No." He was happy to let the boy chatter, growing more confident, but he needed to make him focus. "Food. Water."

"Ah. Right. Well, just hang on. I'll pop home for a bit of something. Stay there."

"Good boy. Don't tell anyone. They would make me leave, and go on walking, and I'm too tired and ill to go anywhere."

As the boy started to move away, Vadigan said, "What are those things you hold up to your ears, and talk into?"

The boy looked shocked. "Do you mean mobile telephones? They've been around for years, just much smaller now."

"What do they do?"

"Well, they're telephones."

Tired, ill and irritable, Vadigan snapped, "I don't know what a telephone is! Tell me."

The boy looked nervous now. "It's a thing for talking to people far away. It used to use wires, but now it uses satellite beams."

Incomprehensible gibberish. "Show me."

The boy approached cautiously, and showed him the screen and the keypad. He sent a message to one of his friends, and Vadigan watched in amazement as the reply appeared. Horror at such an obviously evil contraption struggled with fascination at such a wonderful thing.

"Thank you," he said. "Now, please go for food."

While he was gone, Vadigan considered his options. He didn't want to *ask* a small boy to do things for him; small boys were to be told what to do, and smacked on the head when they didn't do it well. On the other hand, things were far from usual. The time, the place, the simple circumstances. He would make as much use of this boy as possible; then, if necessary, he'd kill him. He wanted to move stealthily through this problem, not have his presence blabbed all over.

He wriggled out of the bush, and crouched. Now, he could see the approach of the boy, and anyone else.

The boy was soon back. "That was quick," Vadigan said.

"I live just over there," the boy said, pointing.

"Let me see." He stayed in the crouch, hoping to look less intimidating. "What's your name?"

"Robin. As in Hood."

"Ah," Vadigan said, having no idea what he meant. "So, point me your house, Robin."

"That one, with the blue door. Number twenty four, Belton Road."

For the first time, Vadigan saw the town in the light. He gasped. It was so strange, so big, although the row of terraced houses in which Robin lived was reassuringly small. In front of the houses, a car and a van passed each other. He understood the strange noises now. Carts without horses! More devilry.

But what was *that*? That monstrous edifice?

"That's Bendall House," Robin informed him. "Just apartments. Bit of an eyesore, but people have to live somewhere, they say, so they build those things."

"Where is this place?"

Robin looked at him curiously. "Oxford, of course. Where did you think it was?"

Oxford! After a moment of shock, Vadigan thought clearly. Where else indeed! He had merely travelled through time, not gone anywhere. *Concentrate*! he told himself sternly. Those things aren't relevant. The future is preposterous, hideously ugly. Leave it at that.

"So, you live there with your family."

"Yes. Well, just Mum and Dad. It'd be very crowded if we had any more. Dad says there isn't even room for a dog, which is a shame. I'd like a dog."

"And where are they now? Working for ….a farmer?"

"No," Robin laughed. "A farmer? The nearest one is about twenty miles away. Dad works in the council office, and Mum works in a computer firm."

"The woman works?"

"Yes. Most of them do."

"What … year is this?"

Robin looked at him. "You don't know what year it is? Have you been having too much of the dangerous stuff? Drinking it or smoking it?"

"I'm … old and I've been ill. My memory sometimes fails."

Robin told him the year, adding, "16ᵗʰ of October."

"So," Vadigan said, "What do you do? Do you work?"

"Only in the house. I go to school until four o'clock. Then, I come home, have a play, see who's around, then go in, do a bit of homework until Mum and Dad come home, and have my tea."

The words constantly flitted about Vadigan. He grabbed what seemed to be relevant ones and based his responses on them.

"So, you arrive first, go in, and they come later."

"Yes. They work long hours, and then there's the travelling.

Always slow traffic. I'm lucky. We all set off together, but I just walk to school. They leave a key under … in a hiding place."

"So, your little houses have locks. Very wise to keep the key secret. Don't trust anyone. Thieves and beggars are always passing through."

Seeing Robin looking puzzled, he said quickly, "Well, I'm going to enjoy this. Perhaps I'll see you tomorrow, but I might move on. Don't tell people about me. They suspect strangers."

"Right," said Robin, pleased to be trusted with the secret. "I'll be off, then, Enjoy your meal."

Vadigan looked with distaste at his cheese sandwich. He poked the rubbery bread a few times and sighed. Oh, well. It was food. He chewed some of it slowly, and experimentally turned the top of the bottle of fizzy water.

He jolted in alarm when the water hissed and surged out of the bottle.

When he had eaten the sandwiches and drunk what was left of the water, he lay back and made his plans for the next day.

It was going to be a busy one.

CHAPTER EIGHT

"Come *on*, Robin!"

Mrs Bell trusted her son to be in the house later, after school, but she didn't trust him with leaving it. Too much potential for things left on or open. Once, he had even forgotten to lock the front door. As she might have written on a report card: generally reliable, with alarming lapses.

He arrived at the front door, ready to go. She held out his homework. "Ah," he said brightly. "Thanks. I was just about to fetch that."

She raised an eyebrow.

"Let's go," Mr Bell said, having run the car for a while to de-mist it. Driving through heavy traffic, in the dark, with poor visibility, was his nomination for worst possible start to any day. He envied his son, who was setting off on his short walk to school.

As the car moved away, emitting a thin cloud which hung in the cold air, Vadigan stepped back behind the bush across the road. He thought he was going to vomit. The air in the future world seemed to be scratching his lungs, and his eyes were constantly prickling. But he must keep going, unless he was just going to succumb and die here. Now, that is.

He hurried across the road, glad of the wintery darkness, and stopped at the front door. Robin had said, started to say, that the key was under something. A large plant pot next to the step looked likely. The key was there, very small, as was the keyhole. But seconds later, he was in the warm fug of the house.

He didn't know anything about lighting, so would have to work in the dark until light came from outside. First, he tried to make himself familiar with everything, concentrating on what things were and what they contained, instead of being distracted by unfamiliar appearances and functions.

Soon, the darkness lifted, and he could set to work properly. In the kitchen, he made a small pile of pies, cakes and rolls. Also, some fruit. There was another bottle of the exploding water. There were odd, shiny bags which felt very unpleasant, but would be useful for carrying the food and drink.

In the bedrooms, the more important work began. Clothes. Mr Bell had plenty of them, clothes for all seasons, and various hats. And in another wardrobe, there was a small suitcase. He made a pile on one of the beds, then went into the bathroom. Such a small room but with so many baffling things. He worked out how to use one of Mr Bell's razors, and with a pair of scissors, trimmed his hair, taking care not to drop tufts in the sink or on the floor. All the time, he worked quickly, deftly, not questioning things, not pausing to wonder at them. He was creating a man who could walk confidently about, not being noticed.

He was fascinated by the mirrors all over the place. The first time that he confronted his reflection, he drew back, thinking that some one was standing in front of him. He had often seen mirrors before, but not small ones which suddenly appeared in front of him.

After putting on such clothes as seemed to be an adult

version of Robin's attire, he put his cloak and undergarments in
the small suitcase, with his hat. In a cupboard within Mr Bell's
wardrobe, there was a collection of clothing items which Mr Bell
kept as family mementoes. A trilby hat appealed to Vadigan as
looking respectable. It fitted reasonably well. When he looked at
himself in a full-length mirror, he was pleased with the effect. A
large, double-breasted overcoat, completed his appearance, and
would keep him warm.

Then he noticed the books on a shelf. They would be useful
in his learning the language, and the ways of these people. He
took three paperbacks.

He was about to leave when he saw a wallet on the dressing
table. Inside were various plastic cards, but also pieces of paper
which were probably money, judging by all the wavy lines, and
the picture of someone with a crown. He immediately became
greedy, and went through the whole house, looking for more.
There were no more wallets, but there were coins here and there.
They seemed too light to have much value, but they were clearly
some form of money.

Clothes, money, food and water. He was all set.

He put his bag of food into the suitcase, glanced outside,
then closed the door, replacing the key, and walked quickly
away.

Mr Smythe was already working in his small
pharmacy, being busy, even though his customers were dwin-
dling, leaving only the old and loyal. So far, the big companies
had ignored his little place, but one day, they would come. Like
great vultures, they would descend on him, encircling their
wings round him, and pecking callously through the remnants
of his small business.

His door was still locked, and the 'closed' sign was clear, but old people often ignored time and signs, and expected him to be open. When Vadigan pulled and pushed at the door, clearly becoming irritated, Mr Smythe merely tutted, and went to let the customer in. It was benevolence and business. He wasn't in a position to turn away customers who happened to be a few minutes early.

"Yes, sir. What can I do for you."

The man coughed and shook his head. "Chest," he said. "Bad chest."

"Ah," said Mr Smythe. "There's a lot of it about in this weather. Congested?"

Vadigan nodded. Mr Smythe asked more questions. Vadigan continued to nod, risking an occasional *yes*. Eventually, the chemist passed across a bottle and some chest and vitamin lozenges. Vadigan took out the wallet and gave him a note.

Mr Smythe looked disappointed. "Twenty? Have you nothing smaller?"

Vadigan offered a coin. Mr Smythe rolled his eyes. "Very funny. Never mind. I'll see what I can do."

He rummaged in various places, and counted out the change for his customer, notes and coins. Vadigan looked pleased. He put the money in one coat pocket, and the purchases in another.

Vadigan abruptly left the shop. He was from a time and a social status in which senior officials did not bother with courtesies towards minor tradesmen. But almost immediately, he returned. He held out the bottle, spread his hands and shook his head.

Mr Smythe was a patient man. He said, "Yes, they are tricky. Let me have it and I'll do it for you. You have to press down and twist, like this. Then screw back in the usual way."

Vadigan nodded and left again. He swigged some of the medicine, decided that he'd had much worse, and screwed the lid back on. He sucked a lozenge, which also had a pleasant taste.

The chemist shop was in a side street. Ahead, he could hear a pulsating murmuring. When he turned a corner, he became aware of the cause of the noise. Cars, lorries, buses, swept past, rumbling and growling. This was the worst thing yet. They were like savage monsters, fiery dragons. In the grey gloom, some had their headlights on, making gleaming eyes. He stood staring. Other people stood on each side of him, as though they shared his terror.

"So this," he said, "is how it happens. So many bad people that instead of people going to hell, hell has come to the people. I'm in hell!" In his horror, he cried out, "Hell on earth!"

"Certainly is," chuckled someone beside him. "Uh, there's the little green man."

The monsters stopped, panting, there was a high-pitched beeping as people crossed the road. Vadigan hurried across, whirling round, looking for the little green man, determined to avoid him.

There were faces in the monsters. Were they really travellers, or had they been swallowed, looking out from the jaws?

A man brushed heavily against him, muttering, "Pardon me!" as he blundered through the fog.

"Too late for that," Vadigan called after him.

But was it too late for *him*? He needed to go back. But the way was in that hideously screaming girl's bedroom, or by means of the book, provided that he could build his own from what was in the book.

How could he do that?

He had observed Bacon's instruments, his vessels, his chemicals. He had slipped into the room when Bacon was out. He had stolen notes. And before he had been called to his church vocation, he had received some training in these infernal dabblings.

He became aware that he had wandered away from the scurrying crowds.

A few paces in front of him, a car door swung open. A woman came out of a building. From inside the car, a man's voice called, "Hurry up. If I'm late, he'll kill me."

He? Someone could be killed for being late? At least they still had *some* standards here. Now. But who had this power? One man alone, or was the Church still controlling people's lives in every respect.

But for being late?

The woman slid into the car, and it roared away.

lHe stopped and made himself think slowly and carefully. The monsters were just conveyances, he told himself. Just carts and waggons of the future. That's all. And all this filthy, noisy horror was nothing more than the future.

But if this was the result of sin, could he change it all by terminating and destroying those infernal experiments? Would another come to take Bacon's place? All the books of science must be destroyed. Knowledge was the danger. All it did was lead people astray into sin. All people needed was belief in what they were told by people such as he, and faith. Teach them to read The Bible, and nothing else.

Minutes later, he stood opposite the house which he had left so suddenly a while ago. The house where the girl lived. The house where the book must be, at least some of the time. He could watch the house and find out when it was empty, but that would mean the passing of more time. He had already been away from his own time for too long, he was constantly exposed to this foul air, and Robin's parents might soon discover the loss of the things that he'd taken; and they might extract a confession from Robin. He might even blurt it out. What could be more suspicious than a dishevelled old stranger, begging for food?

It was too light now. These houses weren't joined, but they

were still small and close to one another, and with little foliage to conceal him. Just standing here might look suspicious. He walked briskly away.

He needed an empty house in the dark, or he needed the girl.

The book was either in the house or with the girl.

He would be subtle and cunning, but only up to a point. He would do whatever was necessary to have the book.

He would do anything.

CHAPTER NINE

"Yes, Edie." Mr Reynolds was responding to the raised hand and puzzled frown. His hopes weren't high that this would be a question concerning one of the technical points of this science lesson.

He was right. "Where," she asked, "do you obtain all your equipment? I mean the test tubes, phials, jars and so on."

"I don't. The school does all that for me."

"Then, same question, school instead of you."

"From the suppliers of educational equipment. The school has catalogues and orders from those, as required."

Edie considered this. "But what if, for example, during an important experiment, there was an accident, and some equipment was broken. Glass is easily broken, especially with children involved."

"I doubt that any school experiment would be that urgent. I have not been aware of any strong desire to learn from my lessons. However, while awaiting the provision of replacement equipment, I might be able to manage with my small collection of spares which are in my locked cupboard."

"Ah," Edie said, as though a very large penny had dropped. "So, if someone, say a mad scientist, wanting to destroy the world, or whatever, wanted to steal equipment, there would be three places: the supplier, this room, your cupboard."

The line of questioning hadn't been entirely satisfactory; now, it had plunged into the usual pupil silliness. "Yes," he replied tersely. "It would appear that your statement is correct. Now, having satisfied you on that point, may I continue with the lesson?"

"Yes, sir. Thank you, sir."

Mr Reynolds, the subject, the whole class, dissolved into a peripheral vagueness as Edie thought about the much more important matter of Vadigan's probable intention to conduct his own experiment, then return with the book, and then destroy the book. Probably, Mr Bacon's equipment. Possibly even Mr Bacon.

When she reported to Nico at break, he said, "Yes, that's useful information, although there are other sources. Laboratories, for one. There's a pharmaceutical research place up at Trym Park."

"Yes, but he'd have to find it, travel to it, and presumably go through some pretty intense security."

"True. This place would be much more practical, especially as he's probably been doing surveillance, watching you go to school and back."

Edie shivered and glanced over her shoulder. "That's not a nice thought."

"None of it's *nice*, Edie. And if I were this Vadigan, I'd be following you because you have the book, and I'd be aware of the potential for equipment in the school."

"Really? He's come from a thousand years ago. I doubt that they had schools with well-equipped science blocks. Children's education probably went as far as milking cows and making butter."

"Well, yes. But bear in mind that this guy is going to have to learn very quickly, or he'll be in danger of being completely cut off in this world. And more than that. Remember what I said about the air and germs. And he'll have to find food, and eat that, which his body won't like. He might already be going the way of the Martians."

"It might be insensitive to say it, but I hope so."

"There you are. We've moved on to cheery thoughts of Vadigan turning into a decaying mess, being pecked at by birds."

"Yes. But somehow, I doubt it."

"Somehow, so do I."

*   *   *

"What's in the bag, Ed?"

"Nothing to interest you. School books."

"You seem to be guarding it like there's something valuable in there."

"Just school books."

"Or something you don't want Mum and Dad to see."

"Mum! Do something with him!"

Don't call your sister 'Ed'. You know she doesn't like it.

Edie growled her frustration. "That's the second reason. The first one is that it isn't my name."

Her mother did her neutral look. "Neither is Edie, come to that."

Edie gulped, groaned and sighed, all together. "What a family. I feel like an unwelcome visitor who should be going home soon, to everyone's relief."

"Yup," said Hanny triumphantly. "That's about it, Eddie."

"Hanny, that's not nice."

So tepid. "Well, a little more feeling would have been appropriate. How about you, Dad? Anything to contribute?"

"No. I keep well away from these bickering sessions. I've been working hard all day and want to rest."

Edie's mother bristled. "And I *haven't* been working hard all day?"

"Ha," Edie said. "Like it or not, you're in it now. The whole family arguing, all because of this rotten apple which you keep doing nothing about. Well, I'm off to bedroom sanctuary."

She took a few steps, then lunged back for her bag.

"Yes, don't forget that," Hanny smirked. "Keep your naughty secret safe."

"I don't have a naughty secret."

"No love letters from your boyfriend?"

This time, being on her way out, she ignored him. But as she went up the stairs, she was pleased to hear something being dropped, followed by a bad word from Hanny, followed by a rare joint reprimand by his parents. Edie smiled.

She sat at her desk and took out her school books. She looked at the space where the great thing happened, wanting, not wanting, to see it; and she glanced at the window, half-expecting the tall figure of Vadigan to appear. Thinking of that, she went to look out and confirm what she knew. Not far from her window was a drainpipe, which wouldn't be much of a challenge for a man who could leap through a small sphere into the future, and out of her window and down to the ground without breaking a few legs.

She gazed out into the darkness, thinking, almost *knowing*, that he was out there, plotting and preparing for his attack. He might be ill, cold, hungry, but she doubted that such obstacles would hold him back for long. He looked as though he was made of flexible iron, someone who would stride snarling through disease, hunger and thirst, and even the cold of late

October nights. The man already *was* cold. He would barely notice the temperature outside him.

She turned and looked again at the place where the sphere appeared. In the midst of all the excitement and confusion, she hadn't fully grasped the immensity of what had happened. *She*, Edie Harrison, had seen, apparently a few feet away, through a sort of link, a man called Roger Bacon, from eight hundred or so years ago. And another man, Vadigan, from the same time, had reached through and grabbed her. And she had pushed him away. Then, the first man had thrown a book through to her. And the second man had come through the link, and was determined to have the book.

And now, presumably, in addition to all the other complications, there was a sort of impasse, or stand-off, in which Mr Bacon wouldn't want to connect again because he didn't want Vadigan back, and Vadigan doubly wanted the book, to destroy it, but *after* he had used it to return to his own time.

It was probably accurate to say that she, an entirely innocent party, was stuck right in the middle of the drama.

And she didn't like it one bit.

CHAPTER TEN

TIM WORSLEY LIKED TO VISIT THE OLD, DILAPIDATED, reputedly haunted house in Crescent Road. At dusk. Doing it in the dark was too much. Anyway, he wasn't allowed out on his own after dark.

He didn't exactly visit the house: he liked to stand in the road and enjoy being afraid. He liked to think about going up, and into, the house. He liked to imagine going up the rickety, dusty stairs, walking slowly up through the gloom, intrepid, a firm challenge to anyone or anything in the house.

He liked to imagine not being afraid.

But never for long. There was always a sudden flickering of the darkness, fleeting shadows flitting across cracked and filthy windows. Sometimes, there was even a creaking or a clumping as the wind grew stronger.

He'd had enough of a thrill for today.

He turned, and cried out as he saw someone standing behind him.

In front of him now.

A tall man who looked down sternly.

"Alone?" asked the man. "Here?"

"Yes. It's out of bounds. Police, parents, council. They all say we must keep away. It's dangerous."

"Why is it dangerous?"

"They say danger from falling things."

Vadigan nodded shrewdly. "That is likely. It does look dangerous."

Reassured, Tim said confidentially, "And people say it's *haunted*. People have seen *ghosts*. People have run out of there, terrified because they've seen ghosts."

"There is only one ghost of which you need be afraid! The Holy Ghost."

As the boy flinched, Vadigan controlled himself and returned to practicalities. "But I have heard of demons that cling to old buildings, miserable wretches who don't want to leave, and who take revenge on anyone who enters, blaming them for their sorrow. I can feel the evil, even from here. Yes, you would do well to stay away from that place. Tell your friends to stay away, too."

"Yes. I shall." Tim's eyes were wide. He was afraid.

"Run along, then," said Vadigan softly. "Play in the pleasant places, well away from all that crumbling darkness and misery."

Vadigan had decided that the ruined house would be suitable for his temporary residence and workshop. His conversation with the boy had encouraged him. He'd be away from prying eyes. And anyone who did come for a peep might see a ghostly figure in there. He almost chuckled. The old superstitions of the peasants might be useful to him.

He glanced round. No-one was in sight. The old house had no neighbours and was well-screened by large bushes. A sign which stated 'Site Acquired for Development' made it clear to present day people what was going to happen; but Vadigan had seen enough to have a rough idea of what was intended. Well, they could do what they wanted, so long as he had a few days in which to do what he needed to do.

He walked quickly along the overgrown path to the front door. It was closed, locked and padlocked. A quick inspection of the windows showed the uselessness of the front door security. With a quick twist of his strong hands, he pulled away a section of the hardboard which covered the window. He threw in his suitcase and leapt nimbly onto the window sill and down the other side, crunching on broken glass.

As he looked into the gloom, Vadigan wasn't bothered about the dismal darkness. For one thing, he came from a time in which there was little light apart from the sun and candles, and he spent a lot of his time groping through the dark and chilly passages of churches. For another, he was Vadigan, a man of religious purity, who spread fear, who wasn't afraid. Even so, he opened his suitcase and felt the implements which he had bought today from the ironmongery section of a large shop. A hammer, a chisel, and, now gripped firmly in case of physical danger, an axe. He didn't like its design of steel and rubber, but he approved of the sharp blade.

As he didn't want to keep coming and going through a window, he went to the front door, and soon had it open. The padlock was strong, but the wood into which it was fastened was weak. A moral lesson there, he thought. After ensuring that the door could be opened wide enough for his thin body, he pushed it shut again.

As he wandered through the rooms, he realised the problem of setting up and using the equipment. This was not going to be easy. The roof, ceilings and parts of the walls and floors, had collapsed. Beams and shards of plaster hung precariously. This was certainly a place to be avoided. Exactly what he needed for secrecy, but not for conducting experiments.

Then, there was the very significant matter of the various chemicals, which had to found, bought or stolen, and carefully measured, in this dark and dirty place.

And, of course, he needed the book.

* * *

ROBIN KNEW THAT HE WAS GOING TO BE IN TROUBLE, AS soon as his parents began to go round the rooms upstairs, exclaiming loudly about missing items. He sat and listened anxiously as the exclamations became louder and angrier.

"Well, that's typical," bellowed Mr Bell. "I just happened to draw out all the money for the plumber's job. How, why? *Why?*"

He came downstairs, opened the front door and looked at it, looked at the windows, looked at the back door, and announced, "Whoever it was didn't break in. The thief just walked in."

Coming downstairs, Mrs Bell said, "Well, it was a silly place to leave the key. Everyone knows it's a traditional place, especially the thieves."

"It's supposed to be a respectable neighbourhood."

"That's where the thieves go. More chance of money."

"Well, they certainly found it here. And clothes."

"And food. I didn't think anything of it at the time, but there's food missing."

Mr Bell raised his arms in a vague gesture. "Well, *haven't* we been helpful. The key in an obvious place, money, clothes, food, all there for the taking."

"We must put a stop on the cards, tell the police, and look for someone wearing your best suit and coat."

"And my dad's trilby." He looked at his silent son. "Robin, have you told anyone where we keep the key?"

"No."

"Sure? You won't be in trouble, but if you've told anyone, we need to know. The police will need to know."

"No, I haven't told anyone."

"Okay."

The evening passed very slowly for Robin, dragging its great weight of knowledge and deceit. The evening meal and supper seemed to join each other somewhere in Robin's chest, as though refusing to go anywhere until he had told the truth. He tried to reassure himself that he hadn't actually told that man where the key was, and that it wasn't necessarily the man who had done it; but he knew that he was …. concealing vital evidence; that's what they called it.

Sleep refused to cooperate, too. It seemed as though everything was sitting in moral judgment on him. He heard his parents go to bed, and told himself that it was late, there was school tomorrow and he must sleep.

But still it didn't happen. Clocks ticked, and a big one in the town tolled mournfully, as though it was the day of his execution.

When the dongs had stopped, and a brief silence descended, he tried again.

It was no use. He pushed back his duvet, wriggled his feet into his slippers and padded over the landing to his parents' room. He tapped on the door and eased it open.

"Mum? Dad?" he said into the darkness.

"When he said it again, there was some mumbling, and his mother said, "Robin? What is it?"

Beside her he saw the dark shape of his father turn into a sitting position. As Robin hesitated, he said, "What is it? Don't you feel well?"

Irrelevantly, Robin said, "No. I mean, yes. Yes, I don't not feel well. I mean …"

"Robin," Mrs Bell said, wearily. "It's very late, or very early, depending on how you look at it ..."

"Don't you start," Mr Bell said, grumpily. "Robin! What's the matter?"

"Well, I might have *nearly* told someone where the key is kept."

CHAPTER ELEVEN

THE LIBRARY WAS QUIET, AS LIBRARIES USUALLY ARE. MISS Tennent was accepting the payment of a fine, and expected that to be the highest level of animation for the day. It wasn't an exciting life, and she preferred it that way. She was far from being a stereotypical old spinster, but she liked to have her excitement well away from the place where she earned her salary. Her private life, with music and painting, and exploratory holidays to faraway places, was her real life; this was merely the place where, as it were, she collected the money to pay for her interests. She enjoyed reading books, but she did not enjoy putting them into categories for sections and shelves.

Mr Trumble paid his fine with his usual stoical acceptance of a system which frequently defeated him, but which he had to admit was perfectly simple and fair. As he left, he might have noticed a tall, dour man entering the library, but it would have been in a vague, peripheral way. Miss Tennent did see him, but in the same way. Just another person entering in the pursuit of books. But she certainly noticed the rather aggressive way in which he strode about selecting and rejecting books, with snappish grunts and exclamations of distaste.

He was selecting a lot of books, filling his long arms with well above the maximum permitted number.

There was something … dark about him. A sort of dark aura. No colour, unless it were a deep shade of grey, verging on black. He seemed to have brought in his own little weather system of gloominess. She wasn't looking forward to telling him that some of his books would have to be put back on their shelves. She tried to immerse herself in the problem of trying to decide in which category 1984 should go, but she kept glancing at the man with his arms full of books. When he turned and began to walk towards her, she felt the same despair that George Orwell's little man felt.

When the man arrived at the counter, he dropped the books on it and said, "What is the cost?"

Miss Tennent blinked. She knew that wasn't an adequate response to the question, but it was such an odd and unexpected question that she didn't know how to reply.

"What is the cost of what?" was all she could manage.

His frown sharpened. "The books," he said tersely. "I want to purchase these books."

"But we don't sell books."

"Come, woman! This is a bookshop, is it not?"

"No. It's a library."

"Libraria. A bookshop."

"No. A library."

Vadigan stepped back, spread his arms and rolled his eyes. "Look around you, woman! What do you see? Books. Thousands of them. What you would expect to see in a bookshop. So, this is a bookshop, and I wish to purchase these books. Are you going to sell these books to me?"

"I can't. We don't."

"Why not?"

"We'll lend them to you."

"Lend? What do you mean?"

"We give them to you, you read them, then bring them back. That's how libraries work."

She watched him thinking about this. Equal measures of distaste and consideration passed across his face.

"When must they be returned?"

"Three weeks, or earlier if it suits you."

"Very well," he said. "I hope not to need them for three weeks, so that will be satisfactory."

He began to gather up the books, but Miss Tennent's agile mind was already anticipating the next problem. "But first, you must satisfy the residence test."

"Test? What test?"

"P…proof of residence. You must be living in the district covered by the library."

"I am."

"I need documentary proof, such as a utility bill, addressed to you."

"I have none. No-one writes to me, except the bishop, and occasionally other senior members of the church. And not at my present address, to which I recently came."

"I must have it, I'm afraid."

"Afraid of what? You bewilder me. Is your master here? I shall speak with him."

At that, Miss Tennent drew herself up to slightly more than her full height and said, "*I* am in charge of this library, and *I* administer in strict accordance with the rules. Do you wish to make a complaint? There is a set procedure for doing so."

At last it dawned on Vadigan that a more conciliatory approach was needed. His high social status and authority in his own time had no value here. He needed people to help him. He must ask for that help.

Swallowing his pride, and immediately suffering with indigestion, he said, "I do apologise. I have had a very long journey and have been very ill. I am hoping for some quiet time with some books to aid my recovery. Your refusal made me rather frustrated."

The librarian was easily mollified. She hadn't enjoyed losing her temper, but she was pleased by its effect.

"Right, then. Let's start again and discuss this politely in the hope of finding a solution to our problem. First, what is your name?"

"Vadigan."

"How do you spell that?"

He spelled it for her, but she struggled with the strange pronunciation of the letters. She asked, "Have you been in this country long?"

He was about to respond with his highest haughtiness when his quick brain told him that being mistaken for a foreigner might be a very good thing, now and in the future. It might make people more likely to accept any oddities in his behaviour.

"No, not long," he said, suddenly meek and humble.

"What is your address?"

He knew only one. Robin's. "Twenty four, Belton Road."

She wrote that on her pad, then glanced down at some of the book titles. "Will you understand these technical books?"

"Some of it will be difficult. But I learn quickly."

"I can see that. You are doing very well." She paused. "Look, Mr Vadigan. I'm going to trust you. Do you promise to take good care of these books and to bring them back within three weeks?"

That was an easy one. The question and the woman were of equal irrelevance. "Yes, I do,"

"Okay. Take your books. But don't tell anyone. I don't want this to set a precedent."

He smiled as he gathered the books into his arms again. He intended it to be a warm and friendly smile, but he failed. Just for a moment, Miss Tennent saw the fiendish lust for success, and a chill passed through her.

"Would you like a bag for your books?" she asked, hurrying to the safety of normality.

"That will be useful," he replied.

She foraged under the counter until she found a large, sturdy carrier bag. She put it on the counter, indicating with a nod that he should put the books in. When he had done that, she pulled the handles together, and made another brief gesture to indicate that he should use the handles to carry the books. He took the bag, and without another word or look, he walked out of the library.

"Well," Miss Tennent said to herself. "I did the decent thing, even if it wasn't appreciated." She chuckled and added, "As usual."

CHAPTER TWELVE

"Edie Harrison, to the headmistress's office."

The command rose out of the shuffling muddle of students. Nico looked enquiringly at her. She shrugged. She had no idea. Unless … She didn't know what the fuss was this morning, but people were milling about the entrance to the science block, some calling out to teachers who were refusing to let them enter and refusing to provide a reason.

Could it be coincidence?

On the way to the headmistress, she began to think that it wasn't.

The wondering grew when she was led into Mrs Pigott's office and saw Mr Reynolds also there.

"I'll come straight to the point, Edie," said Mrs Pigott. "What do you know about last night's occurrence?"

At least Edie could delay with an honest response. "I don't even know what it was."

"A break-in. A theft. Various valuable items of laboratory equipment were stolen."

"Isn't there an alarm?"

"For various reasons, the main one being lack of funds, the alarm was not activated. But that is irrelevant. The theft occurred, and I want to know what you know about it."

"Nothing," Edie replied, summoning up a fair bit of genuine indignation, while pushing into the background what she did know about it.

But now Mr Reynolds attacked. "Why, a couple of weeks ago, were you asking me about how to procure laboratory equipment?"

"Because I was interested."

"*Why* were you interested?"

"Because it is a subject which interests me. I have been reading about Roger Bacon and his experiments, and I wondered how scientists who worked alone would obtain equipment."

"But what has Roger Bacon's equipment, hundreds of years ago, to do with our school in the present day?"

"Just the way my mind works, I suppose. I had him going round in my head, and just wondered, without thinking about different times."

Mr Reynolds looked at Mrs Pigott. It was a look which suggested the necessary implementation of instruments of torture. Mrs Pigott took a mental step back and said, "Why have you been reading about Roger Bacon?"

In desperation, Edie decided to inject some credibility. "Nico, my friend, is interested in science *and* history. He was interested and made me interested. He's a good influence in that way."

"So you know nothing about this?"

Time to wrap this up. "Mrs Pigott, Mr Reynolds, do you really think that I am the mastermind of a laboratory equipment theft organisation? Is there even a lucrative market for the stuff? What's a thief going to do with it ... whatever it is ...bunsen burners, glass jars? Is he going to meet someone in a side-street and stealthily show him a glass jar. How much is a glass jar worth? What do …?"

"Yes. All right, Edie. That will do for now. Go to your lesson, unless it's in the science block; in which case, return to the eagerly waiting crowd and wait for further instruction."

"Yes, Miss …is... Pigott …sir, Mr Reynolds." So confusing. Especially with a scrambled brain.

As she walked back, she thought of how everything that happened in this problem had several connected effects. Here she was, hovering on the edge of disgrace at school, and possible arrest by the police, certainly under heavy suspicion all round; and the deeper problem in all this was that Vadigan now had at least some of the equipment that he needed, which meant that he would soon be ready to make another attempt to take the book.

And if he was keeping equipment somewhere, he must now have somewhere to live.

But how?

And where?

"Where?" she asked Nico in the lunch break. The police investigation hadn't taken long after the confession about the alarm system, and the admission that in monetary terms, the thief hadn't taken anything of great value. To the disappointment of all the students, they hadn't summoned a van of white-coated technicians to dust for fingerprints and crawl around outside the science block, looking for footprints.

"Footprints," a policeman responded with some contempt when the question was asked. "You think we should check for footprints in a large school? Think of how many pupils and teachers there are in this place, and, assuming that they all have two feet, double that figure. Then, answer your own question."

The students who were being deprived of their lessons had been ordered to assemble in the main hall, but as usual, with so much confusion, there had been the inevitable leaking of curious students into the crime scene, where they pestered the two policemen with questions and suggestions.

"Well," said Mr Reynolds as the police car departed, "I rather think the children have done us a favour, by encouraging their departure. We may now resume the lessons."

The students were called back from the main hall, and, looking as reluctant as the students, the teachers were called back from the staff room.

To add to the confusion, the bell rang for the change of lessons, requiring much immediate changing of direction, and the inevitable chaos. Everyone was glad when lunch break arrived.

Nico said, "We should be able to work it out. Someone in his situation can't find it easy to set up a laboratory. He'll need space and privacy. We should be able to do it. We must think."

"And perhaps have a look round."

"Yes. That, too. And another thing. Come on."

She followed him over to the science block. He walked slowly round, looking at the windows. On the far side, he stopped and pointed. "Presumably, the police made a note of this."

Edie looked at the clear sign of forced entry. "Not that I know much about these things," Edie said, "but it looks like a neat job."

"Yes. Especially when you consider how unfamiliar all this is for him. He's done just enough to be able to lift the window. He was lucky, though. He wouldn't know about electronic alarms."

"He seems to be a fast learner,"

"Yes, that's true. We'll have to be sharp to stay at least one step ahead of him."

"So far, it looks as though we're several steps behind."

"In that case, let's catch up. We need to think ahead, try to anticipate his moves."

"If he does manage to set up his laboratory and buy, steal or find whatever he needs, I think I know what his next step will be."

Nico gave a little sigh. "Yes, it does seem an obvious one. But, let me think …" He paced about, using his fingers like a conductor's batons. He stopped and said. "Right. I suggest a variation of the hunter and hunted switch. He wants the book for two reasons. He wants to go back, and he wants to destroy it. Our aim, therefore, is to prevent those two things."

"But I want him to go back. I'd be happy for him to destroy the book."

"It's so frustrating. A beautiful event has been ruined by this bad character. You and Mr Bacon could have been doing great things, perhaps dangerous things, in view of all the things that go with tampering with time, but it would have been interesting and worthwhile."

"And Vadigan has spoilt it all."

"In that case, let's punish him. Let's annoy him. We'll do what we can to keep him here, trapped, without a past in the present, if you see what I mean. And he can't immediately learn how to forge documents to create an identity for himself. Perhaps long ago, he could have done it by forging a few documents; but now, the system is too big, too computerised, too centralised. So, all the time that he's stuck in our time, he's running out of time. He has his equipment, he has a place in which to keep it. So what? He still has to find all his ingredients, some of which might no longer exist, or have different names, and he has to be able to make it all work."

"And he might have to do whatever accidental thing we assume Mr Bacon did. Remember, he was surprised and bewildered."

Nico laughed. "He was probably busy doing the old thing of trying to turn base metal into gold, and, whump, he accidentally discovered time travel."

"Yes. But more than time travel: two times existing next to, or within, each other, at the same time."

"And instead of standing back in awestruck admiration, Vadigan wants to destroy it as something unholy."

"I think it's always been the way. Science and religion opposing each other instead of being two connected parts of one thing."

"Very well put. Well, I don't know what part we can play in this never-ending war. We can take the narrow view that it's Vadigan against us, and against Mr Bacon, but there probably isn't much, if anything, that we can do to help our long ago friend."

"All we can do is assume that whatever we do to harm Vadigan will help Mr Bacon."

"Agreed. In which case, I suggest that we work out some sort of plan. You have a big think tonight, and I'll do the same."

"I'll start thinking this afternoon."

"No! Don't muddle lessons with the problem. Concentrate. Besides, thinking of other things for a while might help the other thinking later. And it's important to stay out of trouble. More trouble."

"I'll try."

They started to walk back, when she said, "To move whatever he needs must have taken a few journeys. He *must* be somewhere close."

"So much for thinking of other things. But a very good point."

"And we should be able to work out where it is."

CHAPTER THIRTEEN

HANNY WAS SLOWLY MAKING HIS WAY HOME FROM SCHOOL, kicking stones, treading on beetles, generally enjoying himself after the restraints of school. He was so absorbed that he didn't hear the footsteps behind him. He became aware of the stranger only when he was right beside him, almost walking in step.

"Hello, Hanny, " said the stranger.

"Hello," Hanny said, adding in his forthright way, "I don't talk to strangers."

Vadigan was prepared, He had been reading, absorbing. He was keen to learn new things for his very bad cause. Not otherwise.

"Well, that's probably good advice, generally speaking. But this stranger needs to be talked to, Hanny. You see, I'm a detective. This is confidential, Hanny. You know about the robbery at your school?"

"Yes."

"Some equipment was stolen. Also, a valuable book. Did you know about that?"

"I knew about the other stuff. Not about the book."

"It's a very special book. You might say, a secret book. And, confidentially, Hanny, there is reason to believe that your sister has it."

"Puh. I'm not surprised."

"Why aren't you surprised, Hanny?"

"She's always up to something. And she's been carrying that bag of hers round for days. Before the robbery, in fact."

"Yes," Vadigan said quickly. "The robbery was in two stages. The book was taken first, some days ago."

"Why didn't anyone say anything?"

"Because, as I said, Hanny, the book is a secret, because of its rarity, its value."

"Oh. Right. One of those."

"Now, Hanny. Do you want to help the police?"

"Yes."

"It's a big, important task, and we'll be very grateful to you. You see, we don't want to cause distress, ruin a girl's prospects, upset her family. What we want you to do is carefully remove that book and bring it to me. Do you think you can manage that?"

"It won't be easy. She keeps that bag very close. She takes it everywhere."

"Well, that's where the skill comes in. But if you think it's too difficult, just say and we'll have to try something more direct."

"I can do it. It won't be easy, but I can do it."

"Well done, Hanny. Now, discretion and confidentiality all the way. Don't say anything to anyone. If she catches you taking it, just say you were curious. But if successful, take the book to …"

A glimmer of intelligence. "Hey, aren't you supposed to show me your badge, or something else to confirm who you are?"

"Not in real life, Hanny. What if I were to be killed, with all my verifications on me? Secrecy all the way in our job, Hanny."

"Hm. Suppose so."

"Now, as I was saying. Take the book to the oak tree directly opposite the old haunted house. You know the one I mean?"

"Oh, yes. I know it."

"There is a small hole at the bottom of that tree. Place the book in it. I, or one of my colleagues, will remove it later."

"Okay."

"There will be a reward for doing this important work."

"What? Money?"

"Yes, Hanny. Money. Money for *you*. And a note will be made of your name, for future reference. We're always keen to recruit the right sort. In a few years, of course. But we don't forget, Hanny."

"Right. I don't know when it'll be. She keeps the bag very close."

"Seize the moment, Hanny. Be alert, be ready, and seize the moment."

Hanny put a finger to his forehead in a vague salute that he had seen somewhere, probably in a film. Vadigan imitated the gesture and almost smiled as he watched Hanny continue to his house.

* * *

"Yes?" Edie asked pointedly.

"Nothing," Hanny said, not convincing her of his innocence. "Why?"

"You're staring at me. Watching me."

"That's because you're so beautiful and interesting."

"Don't. Find something to do."

"I try to be nice, and this is what you're like."

Mrs Harrison said distractedly, "Stop bickering, you two."

Edie knew that he wasn't looking at her. He was looking at her bag. He was bursting with curiosity, and his attempts at nonchalance were not impressive. He kept returning to his iPad games, but she could *feel* his attention on her bag. Did he *know* something, or was his curiosity driven by his *not* knowing?

When she went to the bathroom, she listened for any movement in the lounge. When she hurried back, she casually felt inside her bag, relieved to feel the book still in there.

She didn't know that for the first time in his life, Hanny was being cautious and patient. He wasn't going to grab the book at night, when there was nothing that he could do with it, and when the theft would be expected. He needed to carry out the task in one smooth operation, when it wasn't expected. Grab and go, deposit and return. Or carry on to school. That would be the best time, in the morning scramble, when everyone was distracted with meals, washes, shaves, packing lunches.

He went to bed early, giving Edie what he thought was a friendly smile as he passed. She saw a fiendish grin.

Hanny did nothing the next day. He didn't even look at her from start to finish. He'd decided when it was going to be done, and for that, he needed a few moments when Edie was completely off her guard. In the evening, he ignored her and the bag. It was tempting to look at it, and in it, when she popped out, but he resisted. A new Hanny was developing. One who thought. One who plotted.

The next morning, he poured a small helping of cereal and ate slowly, ready to gobble the last bit when it was time to make his move, but not finishing and being ready too soon.

He didn't look at his sister, even when she squirmed and murmured, "Hurry up, Dad. I have to set off soon." He continued to lift small portions of cereal to his mouth, seeming to be eating heartily.

The bathroom door opened. Edie dashed upstairs. Hanny stretched out a leg and pulled Edie's bag beneath him. He lifted out the book, and put it in his own bag. Then he pushed Edie's bag back to where it had been.

He quickly finished his cereal and took his bowl to the sink. As he put it in the soapy water, he called, "I'll be off now."

"Not without brushing your teeth," his dad replied.

Standing by the sink when Edie returned was almost an alibi. He was well away from the bag. But would she still check it before she left? Reminding himself not to be dashing, he went up and brushed his teeth lightly, then walked steadily downstairs.

"Right," he said, picking up his bag. "See you all tonight."

He ambled out and away in his usual languid manner, not looking in any way suspicious. He walked a few steps away from the house, then accelerated into an instant sprint. It wasn't far. A right and a left, across the patchy remains of the village green, along a narrow path, and there it was. One derelict house, and one big tree, which must be the oak tree. The hole wasn't large, but he pushed the book in, and immediately set off for school by an improvised route.

Going by the usual route, Edie was surprised to see him approaching from the right.

"Looking for conkers," he called. "No decent ones."

"Oh."

Why was he bothering to explain?

He even gave her his version of a friendly smile as he walked quickly past. Now, *that* was definitely suspicious. She felt the chill of horror, as she put her bag down and opened it.

In the few moments of rummaging, Hanny was well on the way to the school entrance.

She looked at his departing figure and cried, "Hanny! What have you done? *WHY?*"

She became aware of tears, of rage, frustration and sorrow, pouring down her cheeks.

"Hanny," she cried again. "You little … SOD!"

CHAPTER FOURTEEN

HANNY SMIRKED. HIS EXPRESSION TAUNTED EDIE, SILENTLY saying, 'Go on, then. Tell them. Tell them your secret. You daren't. *I* know the truth, because a detective told me what you've been up to.'

When her parents went out to the kitchen, Edie leaned across the table and said quietly, "Why, Hanny? Why did you steal the book? What good is it to you?"

"It's not for me."

"No. It's for *him*, isn't it, Hanny? What did he tell you?"

"I'm not saying anything. It's secret."

"Of course it is. People who do very bad things like to keep them secret."

"*You're* the one who's doing very bad things."

"Is that what he told you? A stranger told you that I was doing bad things. How did a stranger know?"

"He's a detective."

Bit by bit, she was drawing it out of him. Delicacy and diplomacy instead of confrontation.

"A detective? Well, did he say what bad things I've been doing?"

"You know what they are, because you did them."

"Just tell me what *he* said I've been doing."

"Stealing things. From school. Science things. And the book."

"Right. One last question. Did you give the book to him?"

"I put it in a place that he said."

"Okay. It wasn't the last question. Which place?"

"Secret."

She stood back and drew in a long breath. "I need to know, Hanny. He's a very bad man who is doing dangerous things. He's made use of you. I'm trying to stop him. You could help me. Be a big boy instead of a little one."

She left it there and went up to her room. There was no point in trying to persuade him. She had planted the seed. Now, patience.

Homework and patience.

Drifting and pondering.

Somewhere near. She and Nico had agreed that he was somewhere near.

What was near, and suitable?

That abandoned house?

She heard Hanny coming up the stairs. He went into his room.

She hurried after him, preventing him from closing the door, then closed it behind her. She advanced, and he opened his mouth to yell. Edie flapped a hand and shushed him.

Trying to look not-threatening, she went closer and said, "Was it the abandoned house?"

After a brief, guilty, hesitation, he said, "No."

"Near?"

"It's a secret."

"Hanny. I told you it's time to be a big boy. I can give you a much bigger secret which will show you why this secret must be revealed. It's *my* secret. Only Nico knows. And of course, the bad man. His name is Vadigan."

At least she had his attention. "Come to my room. First, I want to show you something on the computer. That's the background. Then, I'll tell you what's been happening."

She showed him items about Roger Bacon, trod diplomatically through Hanny's inevitable attempts at humour, and emphasised the scientific experiments part of it.

"Right," Hanny said. "So, there's a science guy living thousands of years ago…"

"Hundreds."

"Whatever, and he wrote this book, I presume, and it's bound to be worth a lot of money, which you want, and this other guy has it now, so he'll have the money, and you want the money, so you want the book back…"

"Hanny, you need a brake. I mean the sort that stops you. 'Yes' to 'he wrote this book', and 'this other guy has it now' and 'No' to everything else. Well, the book might be worth a lot of money, but that isn't relevant."

She stalled for a few seconds while she came out of the history pages. Hanny's 'What is, then?" seemed to come from far away. If it weren't for his bit of information, Hanny wouldn't be relevant either.

She turned to face him and said, "Not very long ago, I've lost track of weeks and days, a strange thing happened. One of those strange things that you don't believe when other people tell you. A little way to your left, a fuzzy patch appeared."

"What? On the wall?"

"No. Not *on* anything. It was, well, in the air. Hovering, if you like." She took a deep breath and exhaled. "It formed a sphere. And then a man appeared. He was in what appeared to be a laboratory. Like the one at school."

"I haven't seen the one at school. I'm still in…"

"Well, anyway, a long bench with a row of glass jars, tubes, liquids bubbling and steaming. Well, all that was the first shock. The second was when he looked up at me. He could see me."

"Why looked *up*?"

"Good question. This laboratory seemed to be a bit lower than my bedroom floor. But it was all very clear. The man was very clear. I could see that he was dressed in a monk's habit. Now, I'm going to summarise a little. We held cards up for each other, having written brief messages. I didn't understand his at the time. I didn't know any more about Roger Bacon than you did. But Nico looked them up. He told me that the man was confirming that he was Roger Bacon. It was doubly difficult because he was living in a time when our language was very different, and when much communication was in Latin. Add in the science stuff, and you can see one big problem."

"Could you hear each other?"

"Another good question. No. That's why we used written messages."

"Like sending text messages instead of ringing someone."

"Just like that. Except that this wasn't a matter of choice. Now, if we'd been left alone, we could have made a lot of progress, gradually adapting to each other and our different times. But there was an intrusion. A very nasty man, who clearly disapproved of Mr Bacon's experiments."

"Why?"

"Some people don't see the beauty of God in learning, in asking questions. Let's not go into all that. Just accept that this bad man objected. He tried to climb through, and almost did. Mr Bacon broke some glasses and the sphere faded. The nasty man must have made it clear that he intended to destroy Mr

Bacon's book of notes, and probably all traces of his experiments, because a few days later, the sphere appeared again and the book was thrown through. I understood that I was to keep it safe. As soon as the book was through, the sphere disappeared. It appeared briefly one more time, when I was trying to sleep. The bad man, Vadigan, came through. He was coming towards me when I yelled. Mum and Dad came, and he jumped out of the window and vanished."

Hanny used his gaping mouth for speech. "I remember your screaming. So, why does he want this book?"

"I presume that he wants to destroy it."

"But he has it now. He'll have done what he wanted."

"Not unless he wants to stay in our time. If he wants to go back, he must use the book to make another way back. Then, he'll destroy the book."

"Unless the original sphere comes back."

"Well, first, he'd have to be here when it did appear. And I suspect that Mr Bacon has kept it closed, as it were. He could provide the way back for Vadigan, but as soon as he was back, Vadigan would destroy the book and all the equipment, and possibly have him put in prison. Or worse."

"Well, when Vadigan appears back then, again, this Bacon guy should kill him before he can destroy anything."

"I don't think this Bacon guy would be the sort to kill anyone. Besides, it would be a big risk. Vadigan isn't the minor sort of person who could just disappear."

"Then pay someone else to do it."

"I like your thinking, Hanny. Simple and practical. However, it isn't that bit that we need to bother about … yet. What we must do is find Vadigan, before he manages to make anything, take the book off him, and return it to Mr Bacon."

"Leaving this Vadigan stuck here? And now?"

"That's a difficult one. Mr Bacon won't want him at *his* end, and we don't want him at *this* end. There's also the butterfly effect to consider. He isn't supposed to be here. Now. It's interfering with the historical sequence. It can have consequences spreading through, well, everything."

"So, he *has* to go back."

"Probably. I suspect that there will have to be some sort of bargaining and compromise. There is no record of time travel, so something must have prevented it, in some way, at some stage. However, that is well away from our first tasks."

"Worry about it when we come to it?"

"Something like that. But before all that, there is a very important matter to settle. Are you going to help me?"

"Do you promise that all this is true?"

"Yes."

"What about Mum and Dad?"

"Mums and Dads don't believe weird stuff that might be dangerous for their children. Unless desperate, we'll keep it to ourselves."

"And Nico."

"Yes. He's clever and knows a lot. And he's been slightly involved. But that's it. No more."

"I don't want to be in trouble."

"Hanny, for most of your life you've been horrible to your innocent big sister; now I'm giving you the opportunity to go after a big villain. What do you mean by 'in trouble'? I'm in trouble because of this bad man because he wants, wanted, the book. I'm in trouble at school because they suspect me of being involved in the theft of that science equipment."

"Why?"

"Because I was asking questions about obtaining science equipment. I was trying to work out what Vadigan would do. And in the midst of all this, I've had to keep doing schoolwork, at school and at home, and putting up with insults from you."

"Oh, not *insults*. Just humour. Like that man on television that Dad likes."

"Exactly like that man. Hurtful, callous insults.. But let's leave all that. Talking about it *and* doing it. Are you going to help your big sister?"

"Okay."

"A little firmer. A little stronger. What's the answer?"

"Yes."

"Right. First step. I suspect that he told you to leave the book in a place which would be near where he is staying."

Hanny looked blankly at her. She raised her eyebrows. "Oh," Hanny said. "I see. In a hole in a tree." He paused. "Oh. Opposite the haunted house."

"That fits. I couldn't think of anywhere else. Now, you've confirmed it. So, there he is, in that big house which people are afraid to go in, with the book and the equipment. And he must be stopped."

She looked at Hanny. Deliberately or otherwise, he was now being very obtuse. Edie continued to look, and slowly raised an eyebrow or two.

"Tell the police?" he suggested.

"Nice try," Edie replied. "You know what the police would say if we reported what I've been telling you. You know what our parents would say."

"Well, what's the alternative?" He squirmed in his chair because he could see the answer coming.

"*We* are the alternative, Hanny. We three."

"So what are you and Nico going to do?"

"Still struggling with your sums. Okay, Hanny, I understand you're afraid. I shouldn't expect so much from a little boy. Just promise that you won't go against us, that you won't snitch, that if necessary, you'll cover for us. Will you do that?"

Hanny replied through tears, "I'll help. I just don't want to go in the haunted house."

"Neither do I, so I understand. That's fair enough, Hanny. You can be our outside man."

Hanny liked the sound of that. Impressive, but less dangerous.

Edie was pleased. They were no longer enemies, and Hanny was in the team. Now, it was time to tell Nico that there was a team, and that Hanny was in it.

CHAPTER FIFTEEN

"Perfect timing," Nico whispered as they peeped round the tree and saw Vadigan walking away up the road. He was carrying a large bag. They had come straight from school and immediately decided that the tree where Hanny had hidden the book would be the best initial observation post.

"He could be anyone," Edie said. "I think there's a very old saying that clothes maketh the man. Does he look like a religious fanatic from the thirteenth century?"

"He doesn't look like a religious fanatic from *any* century."

"Which would make anything we said against him seem even more ludicrous. That's why we must do this for ourselves."

"Agreed. Right, Hanny. Are you clear?"

Hanny took out Nico's mobile telephone and stared at it. "Yes. No. It wants your pin."

"2987. Here, I'll write it on your wrist."

"Ow."

"It's a ballpoint. They don't hurt. Anyway, you are now in a wussless zone."

"Our outside man," Edie added.

Hanny was somewhere between swelling with pride and trembling with fear.

Nico took a few steps forward and looked for Vadigan. "No sign," he said. "Come on. Let's do it."

They hurried over the grass and across the road, glanced for a last check, then squeezed through the gate and hurried along the path, dodging the outstretched brambles. Mounting the two steps had a symbolic quality, leading them up to the dramatic moment of entering the house. There was no need to open the door. They pushed it until it was just wide enough, and squeezed through. They stood in the large hall, hesitating before the crumbling, rotting former grandeur.

Edie wrinkled her nose and said, "What a dump."

Nico shrugged. "But very effective security. For him."

"You mean the bad reputation?"

"Yes. This is the first time that I've been in the place."

"It shows what you can do when things change."

"Come on. We must concentrate."

They walked carefully through the broken glass, stone and shattered crockery. Turning right into a large room, they entered what must have been a dining room. The long table was still there, covered by dust and chunks of plaster. On the floor beside it was a shattered chandelier. The high ceiling had collapsed. Edie sighed. "I wonder whether any of this could be repaired and restored."

"Concentrate," Nico said. "Focus."

He went past the end of the table and through double doors into a side room. He immediately called to Edie, who was still gazing at the mess and pondering. She quickly joined him. This had been a room for relaxing, with armchairs. In the middle was a fairly large table, on which stood the glasses,. jars, pots, spatulas, and a bowl of smouldering coals.

"We've found *him*," Edie said, "but not *it*."

"He's probably taken it with him, just in case."

Edie thought back, seeing Vadigan walking along the road. "Yes," she agreed. "He was carrying a large bag, but it wasn't flapping about, as an empty bag would do."

Nico looked at the equipment. "I don't want to be a vandal, but would it be a good thing to destroy his equipment?"

"Yes. But he could obtain more of what he needs."

"It would delay him."

"Yes. I'm not ruling it out. It would delay him, and it would make him very angry. That might be dangerous for us, well, me, but it might make him make mistakes. Attacking me might lead to prison for him."

"That might not be sufficient compensation," Nico said sternly. "I don't want possible danger to you in any part of the plans."

"Thank you, Nico. But we'll have to accept possible danger."

"Okay. I don't want probable danger to you."

"Right. In that case, I came prepared for a subtle approach. It might stop the experiments, or it might … wobble them a bit, not give him the results that he needs."

Nico tilted his head and conducted to encourage her to share the information. "And this is … ?"

"Before I set off for school today, I raided the kitchen. Some dried sage, some cayenne pepper, some tarragon. I thought that if we slipped some of these into his jars, his experiments might not work, but without what we've done being obvious."

"Yes," Nico said, nodding. "I like that. Let's do it. Not too much."

He unscrewed the lids of the jars, and Edie shook a little from each of her packets. Nico shook the jars, and screwed the lids tight again.

Edie's telephone rang. She tapped and whispered, "Hello?"

"He's coming."

"Okay. Where is he?"

"He's there!"

Edie ended the call. They could hear Vadigan crunching through the hall, coming towards the dining room.

"While he's making a noise," Nico said, giving her a nudge and a nod towards another doorway. They moved with large, careful strides, trying to avoid the rubble and other broken things. When they stopped to listen, they heard his footsteps going away. A door opened. Trying to go back through the front door was too big a risk, so they took the opportunity to go deeper into the house.

From the relaxing room, they went into a passage. There were more doors on the right, and stairs on the left.

Nico said, "Stairs in a ruined house aren't recommended."

"We could see and not be seen."

Edie went to the first step and stood on it, bobbing gently up and down. She did the same with the second step. And the third. "Saying, "That will do," she went quickly but gently up the rest of the stairs, two at a time.

With a big sigh, Nico carried on up the stairs. At the top, he saw her, in what had been another room, looking down. She was sanding on a wooden beam. Very carefully, he went to her side and looked down, too. Vadigan was busy with his glasses and jars, bubbling and steaming. He glanced from one item to another, his eyes gleaming triumphantly. Before him, a glowing sphere formed.

"Almost there," he said. "I'm about to accomplish what he did. I'm almost sorry that he must be stopped, and the book and all this destroyed. *He'll* be famous for his other dabblings, but *I*, who was his equal in science, but saved humanity from evil, can never have his fame. Where is the great deed when history will show that it didn't exist?

"I must stop him," Edie muttered. "I must prevent his taking that book back to his own time and destroying it."

"It's a long way down," Nico said.

"Perhaps I could land on him."

"You might land on the hot coals."

Vadigan called, "It is time to leave. You failed!"

Edie jumped.

She didn't bother with correct falling techniques, which never helped. She landed on all fours, rolled once, and stood.

Vadigan dived into the sphere.

Edie dived after him.

CHAPTER SIXTEEN

EDIE WAS NEVER ABLE TO EXPLAIN, OR UNDERSTAND, WHAT happened. So much seemed to happen in an incredibly short time. Seconds, moments, instants, all became useless units of measurement. She seemed to be hurtling forwards and backwards simultaneously. Vadigan's feet were right in front of her, but his top half, looking a long way off, was bending sharply to the left. Then it was coming back and passing her in a snarling blur. Somehow, she did the same thing, without the snarl, and there were his feet again as she followed him.

With a screeching whoosh, she shot out of the sphere, skimmed off Vadigan's back and clattered painfully across the rubble and rubbish on the floor.

"Edie!" Nico gasped, hurrying forwards.

As she struggled to her feet, Vadigan strode towards her, flinging Nico sideways.

"What did you *do*?" he raged. "You meddling dolt. What did you *do*?"

Edie tried to stay calm. "Don't blame me because you made a mess of it. What did *you* do?"

"Everything right. That's what *I* did. You were here when I arrived. You must have meddled."

"I don't even have any idea of how it works, so how could I make it *not* work?"

"I don't know how to build a boat, but I know how to sink one."

"Good point. So, what is the next step?"

"The next step is to prevent any further interference by you."

He took a step forward. So did Nico. Vadigan swung his arm and swept him away. Edie retreated as Vadigan advanced. She stopped when she reached the wall.

"Nowhere else to go," Vadigan said with his version of a smile.

"She doesn't need to," called Nico behind him.

Vadigan spun round, realising his mistake. Nico had struggled over and picked up a piece of rubble, which he held over the equipment. There was no mistaking the determined look in his eyes as he said, "Let us leave safely or I'll destroy it all."

"If you do that, I'll kill both of you, and then I'll start again without hindrance."

"Really, Vadigan? Edie just added a few herbs. You were almost there, ready to return to your time with the book. How long would it take you to start again, with new equipment? How long before the police came looking for you? The murder of children is a very big thing in this time. And you're a stranger, in a strange place. Very conspicuous. There are children out there who know about you. They're watching, ready to run off and tell the police."

"Unless we go out there and tell them not to," Edie added, seeing that Vadigan was in a corner and needed to see a way of escape.

Vadigan sneered. "I can't trust you devil children to do any of the things that you say you will do."

"We aren't devil children. That's what you choose to believe. It makes it easier for you to believe that you're good. I promise not to send all those children out there to the police, and Nico and I won't go to the police. In return, I ask for your promise that you will not harm, or cause harm to, Mr Bacon. Unless we are to stand here for the rest of our lives, we must trust each other."

"No meddling? No interference?"

Edie looked at Nico and said, "Nico and I promise that we shall not meddle or interfere with your equipment again. That makes two promises from me, and one from you."

Vadigan considered. "Very well. You may go."

Nico wasn't happy, but he joined Edie. Without speaking, without looking at each other, they walked through the dust and rubble and out of the house.

Edie paused briefly to send a message. "I'm telling Hanny to meet us in York Road. I don't want Vadigan to see us together."

"Does it matter now?"

He looked at her, understanding the eloquence of her silence. "Do you have a plan?"

She looked at him sharply. "Of course I have a plan. Do you really think I'd give in like that? I promised that I'd tell all the children who were gathered round the house not to go to the police." She raised her voice. "All you children. Don't go to the police." That's Number One promise."

"And Number Two promise? How are you going to deal with that one? We promised that we'd not meddle or interfere…"

"With his equipment. And *we* shan't"

"Well, who…? Oh, no. You wouldn't. He couldn't. *He* wouldn't."

"The alternative is to break my promise."

"Is that worse than sending your little brother to his doom?"

"We'll have to arrange it so he isn't going to his doom."

"Our recent arrangement for ourselves wasn't a success."

"That was a sequence of connecting events, with human errors. Hanny wasn't paying attention and gave us a late warning of Vadigan's approach. I was rash and stupid in trying to follow Vadigan through the sphere. From now on, we must plan everything very carefully, anticipating problems and preparing for them."

"So, an entirely new approach for you."

"Yes. We're going to apply so much brain power that even Mr Bacon would approve.

CHAPTER SEVENTEEN

SLOWLY, PATIENTLY, VADIGAN HAD CAREFULLY REMOVED the ingredients which Edie had added. After the recent occurrence, he knew the importance of precision with the various substances. He and the girl had been turned round and spat out. How close had they been to being torn apart, sent miles or years adrift, or sent to some hideous region of a Godless underworld?

For this slow and careful work, he needed daylight. As soon as the sun rose the next day, and cast a pale beam through the dusty window, he discarded from his brain all thoughts which were not directly connected with the creation of the sphere. In his own time, there were few distractions, few noises, and few people dared to disturb him. It was a time when those who weren't toilers in the fields could be thoroughly absorbed in what they were doing without interruption.

The sun rose, bringing more light, as though it were the personal servant of Vadigan. For those who worked with scythe and spade for the important people, it provided a portion of the same light; a sort of residual light. The celestial guiding beams were for the principal purpose of assisting him.

He didn't whistle or hum as he carried out the delicate work, but he was so engrossed that he did not notice his visitor until there was a crunch in the dining room behind him. He swung round, irritated but alert, ready to hurl himself forward with his brandished hammer. But he stood still, and his hammer remained in his pocket.

"Hello," said the visitor.

Vadigan looked closely, remembered and said, "Little Hanny. My recent helper."

"I want to help you again," said Hanny.

"Won't your parents wonder where you are?"

"No. I told them I was playing with friends all day. I planned it. I want to help you."

"Help me with what?"

"What you wanted the book for. I've been watching, through the window. I saw my sister and her boyfriend make a big mess of things. She's like that. A big nuisance. I want to help."

Vadigan was cautious. If the boy was an enemy of the girl, he didn't want to turn him into an enemy of himself. And a little helper might be useful. For errands. Yes, that could work well.

"What has your sister told you about me?"

"*She* says you're not a detective, you're a bad man, come from long ago to steal that book and harm someone back in your own time, and you're trying to go back to your own time to do it."

"And what do you think about that?"

"You're a time traveller. That's all that matters to me. I'm not interested in the other stuff. Anyway, good and bad are only people's opinions, aren't they?"

Vadigan paused and controlled himself. A lecture on religion would not be of interest to the boy, and would confuse him..

Hanny's simple view of the matter was more useful to Vadigan than having a convert.

"Yes," he said. "That is correct. What I am doing is necessary. I consider it to be good, your sister does not. It does not matter. By helping me, you will be privileged to see something very exciting."

"Time travel?"

"Yes."

"I want to come with you."

"Er, not immediately, Hanny. Its success is not guaranteed. I couldn't risk it. But provided that it works well, then I shall come back for you."

Hanny beamed. "Great. Right. What do you want me to do? Hold a jar while you pour stuff in?"

Vadigan suppressed a shudder. Hanny's eagerness to be involved made him nervous. He had no reason to think that the boys of this time might be any less clumsy than the boys of his own time. Or less noisy. Loud inquisitiveness could be a great hazard when he was trying to measure minute quantities of powders without the assistance of the measuring systems and implements of his time.

"Well, first, Hanny, I need some items for my continued sustenance."

"You mean food?"

"Yes. That is exactly what I mean. Be patient for a few moments while I write what I need."

It took more than a few moments. For a man who was used to pens made out of bird feathers, ballpoint pens were capricious dashers, skimming over the flimsy paper like ducks landing on a frozen pond, and as difficult to control. After several minutes of grunting and gasping, which tried Hanny's slim patience to its limit, Vadigan swung round and thrust the piece of paper at his new assistant.

"No need to rush," Vadigan said hopefully.

"I'll need money," Hanny replied."

"Ah, yes. Er, how much will that cost?"

"No idea. I don't do this sort of shopping. Mum and Dad do it all. Sometimes, Edie does some, they pay her. They think she's mature. I don't know why. If you ask me…"

Although he was playing a part to deceive Vadigan, he was warming to the task and almost regressing into the little horror that he used to be. As proof of enmity, Vadigan was pleased to hear it; as a distraction from his work, he wasn't.

"Hanny! You and I know your worth. That is what matters. Take this, and go and carry out your task."

"Yes, sir," Hanny said, remembering to stick to the script. He gripped the money and scrunched away.

He walked along the road, turned left and leaned against a wall. He took out his telephone and said, "Did you hear all that?"

"Yes," Edie replied. "You did very well, apart from wittering about your sister."

"It fitted the plan to make him trust me. I was just a bit carried away."

"Don't. Concentrate. Now, head for the shops. We'll meet you there and help you with the shopping."

"I can manage."

"I know that. We both do. But we want this to go smoothly. And we want to do a run-through of what's been done so far, and what might happen next."

CHAPTER EIGHTEEN

HANNY PUT THE TWO BAGS OF SHOPPING ON THE FLOOR and said, "There wasn't much change. I had to buy the bags, and some of the things were …"

He stopped when Vadigan hissed at him. Bent over the jars and tubes, delicately sifting specks of powders, Vadigan had no interest in the boy or what he had done for him. His own existence was reduced to what his brain, eyes and fingers could achieve.

Hanny waited. Not with patience, but with the understanding of what was required of him. A vital part of his intense training by Edie and Nico was the instilling in him of his importance. He had been promoted to much more than big boy. He was a good guy spy, and might be a good guy saboteur. They had not kept from him the danger of what he was doing. And they had let him choose. There was no pressure, other than by stirring up his dormant conscience.

He noticed that Vadigan was now wearing a long cloak, which suggested his confidence in soon returning to his own time.

Vadigan turned and said, "I was at a crucial stage. You should always wait until you are addressed."

"Yes, sir."

"Well, Hanny. Did you obtain all the things on the list?"

"Yes."

"Was there enough money?"

"Yes."

"More than enough?"

"Slightly."

Vadigan ended the interrogation by holding out his hand. Hanny passed over the change, having previously extracted what he thought was a reasonable payment for his shopping service. Then, emphasising the conclusion of that service, he said, "Now what shall I do?"

"Well, Hanny. There is nothing specific that I want you to do for a while. I mean with my research. But it would be very helpful if, without being conspicuous, you would stand near the entrance and watch for any approaching people."

"You mean stand guard?"

"Er, yes. That sounds right. Will you do that?"

"That's not exciting. No-one comes here."

"You did. Your sister did. Besides, you won't be guarding against the expected, but against the *un*expected."

"I wanted to help with what you're doing."

"You will, Hanny. I shall be able to do my work without the worry of opposition, of intrusion. I could even say that your work will be vital to what I am doing."

"Okay. I'll do that. But only until I become fed-up."

"Yes, we shall have a meal in a little while."

Hanny approved of the prospect of a meal. He went off through the dining room, across the hall and sat carefully on the splintered remains of a cupboard. Edie and Nico had been adamant about having no communication except through the open call to hear what Vadigan was saying. He said, "I'm just sitting here for a while. I might as well switch off."

"No," Edie said. "Leave it on. Just in case."

"Okay. But you'll be bored. I'm just going to sit here, doing nothing."

"Don't worry about that. We'll take turns."

Hanny tried a different approach. The real reason. "But I want to use it. Messages, games, what's happening, all sorts. I don't want to sit here doing nothing."

Edie spoke firmly. "You are to use it for one purpose only. We don't want him to know about it. For your sake, too."

Nico added, "Those things buzz and beep. And you'd have to change back when he might see what you're doing. No risks, Hanny."

"Okay."

"Good," Edie said. "Now, no more talking."

Seconds later, Hanny was fidgeting. Keeping still and being silent was not his way. He liked company and noise, even if electronic. Confronted with the alternative of complete boredom, he tried to pass the time by being an efficient guard. He stared out through the open door, alert to every sound, almost hoping to detect someone prowling through the weeds.

It didn't last for long. Being alert was very tiring, and tedious. Speaking quietly, he said, "I'm bored. Nothing's happening."

"Something *is* happening. Vadigan is making another sphere."

Less quietly, Hanny said, "But he's made me go out into the hall by the front door. I can't observe and report anything when I can't see it."

"Indeed you can't, Hanny."

Hanny jolted and stiffened. He forced himself to turn and

said, "Hello, Mr Vadigan. Just talking to myself. I was a bit lonely here, on my own, not involved in the work."

Vadigan let the glib explanation wash over him. Then he asked, "And to whom were you going to report your observations?"

"Well, after you've gone, and all this is over, it will be a great thing to tell people about. For history. Or don't you want me to do that?"

Vadigan had to admit that the boy combined stupidity with mental agility. That last question could easily lead to a discussion, distracting from the obvious fact of his having been talking into one of those little magic machines.

But having had the pleasure of letting the boy know that he'd been caught, Vadigan instantly realised the better strategy of pretending that he believed the explanation. If the boy was talking, it was reasonable to suppose that there were people listening. Better to let them think their little plan was working.

"I doubt, Hanny, that anyone would believe you. They might even decide that you were insane. Something to think about, Hanny. However, back to the present, I'm not surprised that you are feeling a little restless and lonely, although I recommend talking to God rather than to yourself. Let's go back to what seems to have been a dining room and have some of that food which you bought."

* * *

"I don't believe him," Edie said. "Whatever else he is, he isn't stupid."

"Perhaps he doesn't know about mobile telephones. Or perhaps he didn't see it, or didn't connect what Hanny was saying with it ..."

"Nico! Look around. What do you see? Half the people walking along are having conversations with them up against their ears. Vadigan has been about. He must have seen and heard, and wondered. I can't think like a man from his time, but I think he wouldn't just accept that he'd seen another odd thing. He'd work out that it was some sort of communication system. He'd be curious about what could be used *by* him or *against* him."

"Hmm, yes I suppose you're right. But that leads us to the difficulty of having to plan what to do while not knowing what he's planning to do. With Hanny, I mean."

"I know. And the good news is the bad news, depending on how you look at it. Hanny is useful to Vadigan, which means he'll keep him alive; but it also means that Hanny is a hostage, to be harmed if we attack."

"Although as you said before, murdering a child is a big offence now. He'd be in very big trouble."

"Provided that he was still here."

"Ah. Yes. Well, it seems to me that we're making a very strong case for doing nothing."

"Which means it's a very strong case for doing *some*thing."

"Does it? I'm not sure about that."

"Nico! We, I, have persuaded Hanny to take a massive risk for *our* cause. Now that he's in danger, it's up to us to rescue him, as soon as we can."

"Oh, well, yes. Of course. I was merely debating it, looking at both sides, stating the simple fact that ..."

"This isn't an intellectual challenge. That's like sending a messenger out to the enemy that's about to attack to tell them that you're not ready yet, so would they mind waiting."

"Yes, but we need a plan. We can't just put our heads down and rush into the house. Well, we *can*, but it would do no good."

"Of course." She stopped and pondered. "But if *one* of us

made a clumsy, noisy entrance, and the other one was already in the house…"

"Wouldn't a clumsy, noisy entrance be a bit obvious?"

"Done subtly."

"A subtly clumsy, noisy entrance. Challenge upon challenge."

"Well, I don't expect him to say, 'Goodness gracious, I wonder who that can be. I'd better go and have a look.' We just need him to be briefly distracted."

"So, we separate, I go in the front, treading on some bits of rubble, subtly, while you go in the back or the side, and make your move, whatever it is, at the precise moment that he's briefly distracted."

"Yes. In a nutshell. Yes."

"It'll need some coordinating."

"We have telephones."

"You mean like, 'I'm right above him. Where are you? Over.' 'I'm just outside the dining room. Prepare to make your move. Over.'?"

"No. We'd have telephones on silent, just sending messages."

Nico drew a big breath. "Okay. That's enough discussion. Let's try your plan."

CHAPTER NINETEEN

"Aren't you hungry?"

Hanny looked at Vadigan, who was nibbling a bit of bread. That didn't look right to Hanny. As a hearty scoffer, it bothered him to see someone nibbling, even an enemy. "Don't you feel well?"

"I am cautious," was the reply. "In my short time in this time, I have seen enough to make me aware of the dangers of various forms of infection from the food and drink."

"Oh, you don't have to worry about that," Hanny said, "There are strict rules about hygiene now. All the food is clean."

"That is the problem. My body is not used to clean food. Cleaning food is unnatural. My body is not used to food which is prepared in grotesquely large shops…"

Hanny was shaking his head. "It's worse than that. It isn't prepared in the supermarkets. They just sell it. It's all prepared on gigantic farms and in gigantic factories. I could show you some things."

"Ah. On that … thing of yours."

"Oh. Yes. That's all I use it for, Looking up things."

"I assumed they were a communication device."

"Oh, some idiots use them for chatting to one another. I just use mine for information. You know, learning about things."

"Ah, I see. Well, as soon as you finish that pie, we can resume our work."

"Am I going to help this time?"

"Yes, Hanny. You're going to be very helpful."

Hanny felt a slight shiver in his back. There was something slightly ominous in the way that Vadigan said that; as though he wanted to tell Hanny the secret while keeping the secret. Hanny ate slowly, but there hadn't been much of the pie left. Vadigan had wrapped the rest of the provisions; the end of the pie meant the end of the meal.

"Ready?" Vadigan asked politely.

"I need the toilet."

Vadigan swept his arm round. "We are in a ruined building. Go where you want."

"No, it's not that."

Vadigan was used to the dirt of his time, but this was new dirt, and he wanted a clean laboratory. He didn't know about germs. For him, it was just different forms of bad air. If he managed to go back, then he, *he*, might be taking this modern sickness back to his own time, where there would be no cure. Not for anyone. Not for him.

Hanny said helpfully, "One of the toilets in the house might be intact. I could go and look for one."

"No. We're too busy to let you go wandering about, possibly into danger. The cellar is the place."

"Where's that?"

"In the hall, turn right, and you will see the door ahead, on your left."

"Right. I shan't be long."

"Oh, Hanny! Do you really think I'm stupid? Do you really think I'd let you go off on your own?"

"Why wouldn't you?"

"Because as soon as you were in the hall, you would turn left instead of right and run away."

"Why would I do that? I chose to come here because I want to help with your work. Why would I run away?"

For a few moments, Vadigan sat gently nodding. Hanny had played it very well. Vadigan had a particular use in mind for Hanny. For that, it would be so much easier to have an acquiescent, docile Hanny than a rebellious, frightened one.

But the latter version was much better than no Hanny at all.

But if he were to go to the cellar door with Hanny, he would have to leave his equipment vulnerable to an attack. And it was almost ready! He looked anxiously up and around. His absence might be a part of the plan, or a new part of it. But even going to check for intruders would mean leaving his equipment exposed.

He decided. "No, Hanny. I didn't express it very well. Remember that your language now is to me what a foreign language is to you. I meant that those people who don't approve of your working with me might order, or entice, you to leave me. I don't want that, and you don't want that. I shall come as far as the hall, from where I shall be able to see both ends of the hall."

"That makes sense," said Hanny, wishing it didn't. He was fed up of all this mental and verbal manoeuvring. As he put it to himself, silently, it was a strain on his brain. He had no illusions about that part of him: it wasn't built for hard work or clever stuff. School kept trying to make it do unreasonable things. If *they* had brains which worked, they'd understand his limitations and stop bothering him.

On the other hand, in the present crisis, he was having to coax some sort of activity out of his brain; not for the benefit of a short-tempered teacher, but to please a ruthless madman. It could even be a matter of life and death.

With his escort close behind him, he walked out of the two rooms and into the hall.

* * *

SLOWLY, PAINFULLY, EDIE CRAWLED OVER THE CREAKING beams in what was left of the top floor of the house. In spite of the urgency, in spite of the danger to herself, she was taking a long route, trying to move gradually, almost silently, to the best position for … well, that part of the plan was rather vague. Something like 'grab Hanny and the book and push Vadigan into the sphere'. Nico had wanted something precise, but she pointed out that she couldn't be precise because she didn't know what was going to happen on the way to the moment when she wanted to be precise. Once again, he gave in; as he did when she insisted on being the one to go into the house. "He's *my* brother," she said, "and it was my plan."

So, here she was, torn to shreds, it seemed, by thick brambles, and stung by particularly nasty nettles, and smeared with mould and dust, and whatever else had accumulated on the bits of wood and plaster on which she crawled. Slowly. If the house had been empty, she would have risked standing and using the rickety beams as a gymnast would. But it wasn't, so she didn't. She carefully eased herself along, inch by inch, even breathing quietly.

Reaching a spot where she had a clear view down through the next floor to the dining room, she felt queasy. The rooms had high ceilings, and it was a long way down. But adding to the nauseous feeling was the sight of Vadigan and Hanny. Wrappers at their feet showed that they had finished their meal. She heard Hanny trying to convince Vadigan that he could be trusted to go to the cellar and back; and she heard Vadigan's smooth explanation of his determination to stand guard.

When they walked away, Edie decided that it was an opportunity for a different sort of risk. She tried to give it careful thought, but she decided that she didn't have time for that. This wasn't planning time: this was doing time. And quickly.

There was no safe way to do this; all she could do was reduce the risk. In one movement, she twisted her body, gripped the edge of the beam and lowered her body as slowly as she could until she was hanging by her fingertips. Then, with a slight push outwards, she dropped. With her arms stretched in front of her, she caught the beam below. The impetus made her legs swing up, almost pulling her off. Instead, she improvised. She used the upward surge of her legs to help her to be where she wanted to be. She twisted again, and her legs thrust her onto the top of the beam.

Below, the crunching of rubble warned her that Vadigan was on his way back. She stretched along the beam, trying to be as thin as possible. She heard Hanny say, "So, how much longer will it be, sir?"

"I have almost completed it," Vadigan replied. "I needed a couple of the items to react with each other. Ah, I see that they have done. We are now at the final stage."

"What do you want me to do, sir?"

"Patience, Hanny. Your moment of great importance approaches. Look! The sphere!"

"So, what are you going to do now, sir?"

"I'm going to test it, Hanny. I'm going to make sure that it works."

He looked up and said, "And your annoying sister can watch it happen."

"Run, Hanny! Run!" Even as she called, she was leaping down to the floor.

As she landed, she saw Vadigan pick Hanny up and hurl him into the sphere.

CHAPTER TWENTY

EDIE WAS VAGUELY AWARE OF NICO'S ANGRY VOICE AS HE strode into the room. "What happened to the plan, Edie?"

"It happened too quickly," she snapped back at him. "There wasn't time to exchange messages. That doesn't matter now."

She became aware that Nico was carrying a large piece of wood, holding it in a striking position. "I can break his legs and destroy his sphere, trapping him here," he said.

"You mustn't," Edie said sadly.

"Why ... oh."

"That's right, you silly boy," Vadigan said. "So stop playing at warriors and put that piece of wood down."

"I can still break your legs, or some other things, and keep you from using the sphere."

Vadigan sighed condescendingly. "This young lady's brother has, I hope, very recently arrived in a time which is going to be very strange and frightening for him. He will need someone to take care of him. Someone who knows both times; a lot of one, a little of the other."

"Why would you take care of him?" Nico asked defiantly.

"I feel no animosity towards Hanny. He was helpful to me, before he was persuaded to be a traitor. Based on my experience when I arrived here, he will soon be very ill. Different air, different notions of what is meant by 'clean', what is meant by 'fresh', how children should be treated. And, of course, he won't understand the language."

Edie said, "Do you promise to take care of him, and send him back?"

"I shall do my utmost to protect him, and to return him before I destroy the book and this devilry for ever."

"Do you promise?"

"Yes."

"I mean an oath before God."

There was brief hesitation before he nodded and said, "Yes."

Nico was shaking his head. "I don't like it. For one thing, for all we know, he has caused the death of Hanny, and he should be arrested and tried here…now …. We're aiding and abetting if we let him escape back to then."

"Arrested and tried for what? Murder or manslaughter? Where is the body? Throwing my brother into the past? Even if anyone believed it, it isn't even an offence, because it's never been done. And meanwhile, Hanny is suffering as he's just said."

"But we'll be letting him go."

"He's come this far because we didn't report it to anyone. Now, he's the only person who can help Hanny. And that's the most important thing."

Vadigan said, "One final thing. Your brother hasn't come straight back, as you did, but that isn't proof of success. When your aim is a hair's breadth inaccurate at the bow, the arrow could go well wide of the target. If any of my measurements should be slightly inaccurate, or if the ingredients have changed too much in all those years, both Hanny and I might be wide of our target by a century, or a thousand miles. We might not arrive at the same place. Or any other thing that could go wrong with this form of transportation."

Then you shouldn't have thrown him in," grumbled Nico. Vadigan shrugged.

As though those possibilities were minor matters, Edie said, "What will happen to the sphere when you have gone?"

"Ah. Well, there, you have the advantage. I can't lock it or destroy it behind me. For one thing, it's impossible; for another, I want it to be working perfectly until I have arrived."

"Until Hanny has arrived safely *back here*," Edie corrected.

"I have promised to do my utmost. That might not be enough."

"Unless he's back here within a few days, I'll go looking for him. And you."

"And I'll be with her," added Nico.

Vadigan smiled whimsically. "I commend your loyalty, both of you. I do hope we shan't all arrive separately, hundreds of years, or miles, apart."

Before the thought had time to settle, he turned abruptly and leapt into the sphere.

And disappeared.

Nico said quietly, "I don't want to add to your troubles, but I must. Now that Hanny has gone, what are you going to tell your parents?"

Edie sagged. "In all the excitement, I forgot about that. I have no …"

CHAPTER TWENTY-ONE

THE FIRST STRANGE THING FOR HANNY WAS THAT HE seemed to hit the ground at a very high speed, but with no impact. Just as he was about to expect the breaking of every bone in his body, or at least a severe winding, he realised that he had merely swapped *there* for *here*. No, that wasn't right. *Then* for *now*.

There hadn't really been any speed, because he hadn't gone anywhere. That feeling of movement was just an illusion, as his brain tried to make sense of what was happening.

The second strange thing was his awareness of having those thoughts. "Must have been the shock," he thought.

The moment of clarity was immediately followed by an an awareness of his helplessness and vulnerability, as he stood looking round him. He was on a patch of rough ground near a river. Two rivers. One on each side. And the ground had a very swampy look. Looking one way, he saw the two rivers become one. If they did that the other way, beyond some buildings, this must be a small island. The buildings looked like small houses, but beyond them was a tall one, looking like a tower, and beyond that was a bridge.

Folly Bridge! He remembered. Edie said that was where the Bacon man lived and worked.

"Stand still, Hanny!"

Even as he spoke, Vadigan was striding towards him. He looked angry. Hanny couldn't assess his mood because he usually looked angry. He decided not to take any chances. He set off running over the rough grass.

"Hanny, you idiotic boy! Stand still! You're about to run into a dangerous swamp, some of it very deep. You need to go left, to the firm ground. But listen, Hanny. You can't manage without me. You'll be very ill, as I was, or killed. Children are not highly valued. Hanny, I promised your sister that I'd take care of you. You need me, Hanny."

Hanny had stopped running. He looked back.

"You promised Edie that you'd take care of me?"

"Yes, Hanny. I made a holy promise to protect you, and to try to send you back to your own time, provided that I am able. You must trust me."

Hanny sighed. Edie and Nico had told him about Vadigan's problems in the new time, and even he could understand that he would have similar problems in *his* new time.

He looked at Vadigan, and past him. Showing faintly from this position was this end of the sphere. He waited as Vadigan approached him, then darted to one side and dashed towards it.

Vadigan moved so quickly, that Hanny was barely aware of it. He went down in the tackle, with the big man on top of him. "No!" Vadigan roared. "You will not!"

Winded and crushed, Hanny managed to say, "I need to see Mr Bacon."

"You will. When I am ready. I want his promise. I can

destroy the book, but he might find another way of pursuing his evil practices."

"You said that you'd protect me."

"So I shall, Hanny. So I shall. After all, you're very useful to me. And I know the perfect place for protecting you. Come with me."

Hanny had no choice but to go with him because he was held very firmly and dragged along. And no-one in this time was going to interfere with a man dragging a boy along, or even beating him. Instead of going to Folly Bridge, they moved left over an area of firm ground, crossed the river by a small bridge and went along a narrow way between leaning, bulging houses, weaving between carts loaded with hay, wool and vegetables.

"Where are we going?" Hanny asked as they turned this way and that along lane after lane, street after street. Vadigan didn't reply.

Hanny wasn't merely afraid: he was feeling very queasy and struggling to breathe because of all the strange odours, contrasting with the streaks of clear air. And was the illness starting? It was all very unsettling. When he sneezed three times, Vadigan said, "Yes, it's starting. The sooner we arrive and give you some medicine, the better."

Hanny hardly noticed the people because of Vadigan's speed. They seemed all to be wearing ragged clothes, often tied with string, and all were busy with carts, brushes, parcels, whatever they were carrying or doing. He could hear a muddled cacophony of hens, dogs, sheep and cows, mingling with the shouts of people.

He had been trying to make a mental note of where they were going as they went steadily away from Folly Bridge, but he was tired, afraid, and he could feel something like a bad cold beginning to clog his head.

Vadigan stopped once, to buy some clothes from a stall. He

pushed Hanny into an alley and said, "You need suitable clothes. Change quickly."

Hanny obeyed, surreptitiously transferring everything from his pockets into the one pocket in the baggy breeches which Vadigan had bought.

The new clothes were very rough, and soon Hanny was itching and scratching. He was almost relieved when Vadigan stopped abruptly and knocked on an oak door. When it was opened, a man in what appeared to be a grey dressing gown looked enquiringly at them. Vadigan spoke to him in what might as well have been a foreign language. The man looked disapprovingly at Hanny, shook his head, and stepped back. Vadigan pushed Hanny through the doorway, into a small hall. The other man went off along a passage.

Vadigan bent down and said quietly, "That man is a monk. This is a monastery. You will stay here until I can arrange things with Mr Bacon. You will live here and work here. As you heard in the doorway, you would not be able to make yourself understood outside, in the short time you will be here. I have told them you have had no education and are mentally deficient. That will explain the language problem. You will be safe here. You will soon learn enough of the language to obey. That is all you will need."

"Obey?" That wasn't one of Hanny's strong points.

"Yes, Hanny. As an oblate, an apprentice monk, you will do all that anyone tells you. Failure to obey will lead immediately to punishment."

"How will all this obeying and punishment be protecting me?"

"You will be protected from harm here."

"The punishment might harm me."

"Only temporarily. Its intention is to teach you. To make you a better person."

Hanny almost screamed, "I don't want to be a better person!"

"Oh, dear." Vadigan waved one of his long fingers." This is why you clearly need to be made a better person. The first step is to *want* to be a better person."

Hanny's recent improvements fell away as though washed off him by heavy rain. In their place stood Hanny the Horrible, bad brother, bad son, bad pupil.

With a shuffling of feet, two monks appeared. There was a brief discussion which Hanny didn't understand, and then he was pushed towards the two men, who looked sternly down at him. One of the monks spoke to him, gripped his shoulder and led him along a dark passage, through a door, and down some steps, into a round chamber, lit by a smouldering brazier. Along the curving wall were large holes. Hanny was thinking that they looked like doorways when he was pushed forward and realised that they were. Still being pushed, he entered a small bare room. There was no window, and no furniture, just a long stone seat projecting from one wall.

The monk spoke to him. Hanny presumed he was telling him that this was to be his bedroom. Instantly forgetting the language problem, he said, "Well, thank you very much. If it's all right with you, I'm not feeling very well, so I'll just a have a little rest. Any blankets, pillows?"

The monks looked shocked and held their their arms out, making crosses with their fingers. Hanny spread his arms to show his innocence. "It's not a big deal," he said. "Just a language difficulty. I'm not a witch. Well, a wizard."

He was grabbed and pulled out of the room and back along the passage as far as an intersection, a sharp left turn into another passage. Up steps, along more passages, still in the grip of the grumpy monk. Hanny decided that optimism just wasn't going to work in this case. Escape was his top priority. No hoping, lots of doing.

Another door was opened, and he was pushed through into a small room, bare but for a large cross on a wall. The door was closed, and he heard a key turning. This was another room without a window, which seemed a pretty sharp comment on the monks. Windows could show them beautiful views of the world. They preferred stone walls.

But the worst thing about all these gloomy passages, and rooms without windows, was the lack of opportunity for escaping. And Hanny was very clear on this matter: he must escape.

CHAPTER TWENTY-TWO

HANNY WAS WOKEN FROM A DEEP, SHORT SLEEP OF exhaustion. He felt ill. He sniffed and coughed.

The germs of this time were at work. Probably strong and stout germs to suit this other age.

"What is it *now*?" he asked irritably. A long day of toiling in the laundry, weak and dizzy, a lot of kneeling in the whatever-it-was in the praying part of this place, and his growing illness, seemed a reasonable cause of exhaustion and irritability. At least the silent kneeling provided an excellent opportunity for politely imploring his greatly-neglected God for a bit of assistance with his present problem. But he needed some more rest. For relief now, and for escaping later.

He hoped the God of whenever-this-was would be sympathetic, and helpful. If these annoying monks were his most devoted servants, *he* might be irritable and unsympathetic, too.

The monk who had woken him was clearly joining in with the general crabbiness. Not bothering with words which wouldn't be understood, he dragged Hanny off the stone bed, and along a now familiar passage, at a brisk rate, in spite of the darkness.

Hanny soon realised he was about to participate in a very early morning, or middle of the night, praying session. Dragged into the prayer room and pushed down onto his knees, he added to his prayer for escape a small one for protection for his young knees on this cold, hard floor.

One hour later, he was pulled back to his cell. "Hey!" he called. "You don't have to be so rough. I *want* to go back to my room."

There was no response.

If God could hear the monks' prayers, Hanny wondered what he thought of these interruptions every few hours. Perhaps *his* rest was constantly being interrupted by praying monks. Perhaps when people thought that God wasn't listening to them, it was just that all the lines were busy. Or he'd switched off.

Even his bed of stone felt comfortable, and he was soon asleep again. When the next interruption came, Hanny snapped, "I know. I'm coming," and rolled off the bed.

It's always assumed that anger is the emotion that more than any other drives away fear. It isn't. It's irritation, especially when it has been simmering for a while. As they hurried along, as though God worked to a timetable and didn't want them to be a few minutes late with their requests, Hanny said, "If you're going to expect another day's work from me, accompanied by a lot of kneeling, you'd better do something impressive in the food line."

The monk scowled down at him and put a finger to his lips. "No, I won't!" Hanny shouted at him. "I need food!" He grabbed the monk's sleeve and made eating gestures at him. The response was another scowl, and a firm tug of Hanny's hair. The monk didn't know that of all the offensive acts against Hanny's body and character, pulling his hair was right at the top of the tree. It hurt, and infuriated him into a frenzy.

But a controlled frenzy. He'd learned that much.

THERE *WAS* FOOD. WELL, THERE WAS THE MONASTERY equivalent: a thick, grey porridge, which had been cooked at some early point in its short and miserable life, and had now settled into a sedentary blob. Hanny looked at it with disgust, and then with a similar disapproval at the wooden spoon which was his sole implement for extracting a morsel of edibility.

He failed. He needed at the bare minimum a sharp knife and a stout fork. The only function that the wooden spoon would perform was that of a bat to push the ball of porridge around the bowl.

Still, Hanny thought, it does move my escape plan from impending to immediate. A lot of unpleasant things were happening here, and so far he had been pretty stoical. But some hardships were not to be borne, by Hanny, and the lack of decent food was definitely one of them. No matter how difficult and dangerous it was, he was going to escape today.

Having decided, he was pleased when he wasn't taken to the laundry to work, and delighted when he was taken to the garden instead. On two sides, the garden was bordered by monastery buildings, and on the other two sides by a wall about twice Hanny's height. In his new mood of determination, that was a minor obstacle. He was brusquely 'introduced' to a guardian monk, and it was obvious from the sharp tone and the finger being aggressively jabbed towards Hanny that the guardian was to be very clear about the new gardener's bad character, and to be on the alert for any attempts to escape.

A quick assessment convinced Hanny that the new monk,

already wheezy and looking tired out from nodding his obedience, would be no danger to his plan, which had already been formed while the insults were being delivered. It pleased him to have been thinking instead of being bothered by insults.

He thought of his behaviour towards his sister, and how she had tried to ignore him, and for the first time in his life, he felt ashamed.

By the most basic and simple sign language, Hanny was told to pull up the weeds. Amongst the rows of vegetables and herbs, there were a lot of weeds, which suited him very well. While the monk read and dozed on a tree stump, Hanny worked hard, removing weeds, and a lot of soil, and adding them to a small heap against one of the walls. Soon, with increasing amounts of soil, it wasn't a small heap. But he was patient, even packing the heap down to make it more firm. There would be no second chance.

By the middle of the afternoon, the heap seemed to be high enough, and with no food to weigh him down, he was ready. He glanced across at the guardian. His eyes were closed, and his chin was on his chest.

Hanny took one precautionary measure: he gripped the wooden rake which he'd seen lying on the path. He took a deep breath, braced himself and began to run.

"Hanny!"

The harsh voice of Vadigan made him lose his step and rhythm. He lurched onto the heap, his left foot sinking slightly, and he knew that the rake was his only hope. He thrust it up to catch on the top of the wall, and climbed, hands only because using his feet would push the rake off the wall. It must hang down. He must shimmy up it.

But he felt too weak.

Pull! It's your only chance!

Vadigan's feet pounded along the path. He could easily reach up and pull Hanny down.

"No!" shouted Vadigan.

"No!" echoed Hanny as he stopped climbing, flung his right leg over the top of the wall, and squirmed over. He heard Vadigan's body thud against the wall, and his hands slap where Hanny's feet had been less than a second earlier.

But he was over.

He dropped down, landing with no injury.

Then he was running, with heavy legs and a tight chest, to anywhere that was away from those people, away from that place.

He hoped that he'd given them all very bad twenty-first century colds.

CHAPTER TWENTY-THREE

THROUGH THE RAPIDLY GROWING HAZE OF SICKNESS, Hanny managed to see clearly two distinct and connected obstacles. The two most desirable options for Hanny were to go back, and into, the sphere, or to find Mr Bacon. As Vadigan would be aware.

And the new, thinking, Hanny saw two, connected, subsidiary problems.

Would he infect Mr Bacon? Presumably, not badly, or it would be recorded. Edie hadn't said that he'd died of ... Hanny's Disease.

If he went back, would he infect his family and friends?

To summarise, was he going to infect the people here with Twenty First Century germs, or was he going to take Thirteenth Century germs back to his own time?

Or both?

He became aware that he was running very slowly, and needed to hide. A nearby waggon loaded with sacks would do for a temporary place while he looked and thought. And talked to himself. He needed some friendly company.

"Right," he said. "This is a problem. No arguing with that. In fact, it's a very big problem. I'm stuck in the wrong time, a very long time ago, where the people might as well be speaking another language, I have a very bad man chasing me, and I'm going down with an illness from some ancient germs, for which the treatment will probably be applying leeches, removing a few pints of my blood, or telling me to lick a toad by the light of a full moon."

He was making himself feel less despondent by chatting, setting out the problems as the first step in an eventual plan. And believing that there would be an eventual plan was essential; otherwise, he might just as well accept defeat.

While he was thinking and talking, he was looking through the spokes of the waggon wheels, knowing that soon, Vadigan would appear. And he did, striding purposefully along, his eyes darting to right and left. Hanny began to doubt the effectiveness of his hiding place.

The doubt was removed by a rough and angry voice behind him. Turning, Hanny saw the inevitable gestures to accompany the voice. A large man was clearly not pleased to see a boy crouching almost under his waggon. Equally clearly, he was not interested in explanations. He took big strides towards Hanny. And it wasn't a good time for Hanny to try to explain. A glance showed that Vadigan had heard the commotion, and was already coming towards the waggon.

Hanny ran.

But even as he forced his legs through the motions of running, he was aware of how short they were at all times, and how heavy they were now. And Vadigan was a tall, strong man who wasn't ill, and had a lot of determination. It was only a matter of seconds. Instinctively, he turned off the road, hoping to find somewhere to hide.

He did it without looking. He ran off the road, into emptiness, then plummeted onto hard ground, then into the slop of a very wet bog. His legs were being sucked down, the rest of him soon to follow. But he was close to firm ground. He managed to pull his body up and scramble out and to the entrance of a small cave under the road. He stood trembling with fear, exhaustion and illness, waiting for Vadigan to come down after him.

A thin, old voice startled him even through his fear. He twitched and looked round. Sitting at one side of the entrance to the cave was an old woman. She spoke again and beckoned, pointing deeper into the cave. Hanny had nothing to lose in doing as she suggested.

He heard Vadigan shouting down. The old woman walked out of the cave and shouted back to him. After a short pause, Vadigan called again. The old woman laughed. Again, Vadigan shouted, and again she replied. There was a last, angry, exclamation, then silence, apart from the background noises of working people and their waggons.

The woman regarded Hanny, putting her head to one side, as though she could hear his thoughts, then spoke to him, in a gentle voice.

And at that point, Hanny collapsed and lost consciousness.

*　*　*

WHEN HE BECAME CONSCIOUS AGAIN, A CLAY CUP WAS being pressed to his lips. He sipped and shuddered. It was very bitter. It was a drink without sugar, and with a lot of things to make it sour and harsh. But with her encouragement, he persevered. When it was finished, he went into a deep sleep.

He woke, very briefly, and wondered whether he had become blind. There was nothing but blackness, so intense that it seemed to be solid, with the weight of the entire universe. The immediate return of sleep seemed to dissolve him into the same intensity.

When he woke again, strong sunlight combined with his recovery to make him feel cheerful again. Whatever was in that drink was very powerful. So, he assumed, was his sleep.

And what was that delicious smell? He raised himself on an elbow and looked round. The old woman was crouched before a small fire and a large pot, stirring with a smooth rhythm, and half-talking, half-singing to herself.

She glanced at him, smiled, and said something. He smiled back and walked towards her. She used her spoon to put some of the contents of the pot into a shallow wooden bowl. It was either a thick soup or a thin stew. He sat on a rock and began to eat. It was delicious, and he realised how hungry he was.

When the bowl was empty, he passed it back to her with nods of approval. She spoke again, and he felt very frustrated. He hadn't been interested in what the monks were saying, but he did want to understand what his rescuer was saying. He was going to have to indulge in the old hand gestures, and somehow tell her what his problem was without actually telling her what his problem was. With a lot of flaps and twiddles, he explained to her that he had been imprisoned in the monastery, been made to work with no food (the porridge having no current relevance and being too much of a challenge to describe with his hands), had escaped, and been pursued by the bad man.

She seemed to understand. She took him to the entrance and directed his attention along the steep bank on which the road stood. She gestured up, then down, then shrugged. Now, he understood. There was no way down, unless one chose to jump into the swamp.

In a moment of inspiration, he felt in his pockets, finding a shopping list from a recent errand, and a pen. The other side of the shopping list was blank. From what he could remember of

Edie's description, he crouched over a rock and drew an old, bearded man in a dressing gown, beside a bench on which stood glasses of various sizes and shapes. He showed this to the woman, then pointed at himself and at the picture. She gave him a puzzled look, looked at the picture again, then back at Hanny. She did this several times, then repeated his gesture, pointing at him, then the picture. He smiled and nodded. She raised her eyebrows, rubbed her chin as though there was a beard there, considered, and wandered away to the darkness at the back of the cave.

He heard her footsteps, going away from him, and unmistakeably up.

Secret steps. How else could she come and go?

He sat down to wait.

* * *

HE ROSE QUICKLY WHEN HE HEARD FOOTSTEPS NEAR THE back of the cave. He was ready to run, even though there was nowhere to go but the swamp. But the man who emerged from the darkness was not Vadigan.

Actually, Hanny thought, his drawing wasn't a bad likeness.

And he felt a small surge of pride that he, the annoying little brother, was actually meeting the great scientist who had suddenly appeared to his sister a while ago.

Mr Bacon put his hands on Hanny's shoulders and said, "Edie?"

Hanny assumed that it was just an abbreviated means of establishing his connection with his sister. He nodded, and said," Yes."

The man turned and gently pulled Hanny with him. He spoke to the woman and put some coins in her hand, with a smile and a firm nod of approval. As he drew level with her,

Hanny gave a small bow and a smile, and said, "Thank you." He didn't know what else to do, and hoped that his small gestures would give meaning to his two words. They seemed to, because she looked at him with a warm intensity.

He was soon in deep darkness again, and he lightly held Mr Bacon's cloak as he followed him up narrow, very uneven steps, beneath a very low roof which caused the tall man to stoop. There was a pause, a sliding of something large, another pause, then they slipped out through a narrow gap. The concealing boulder was slid back into place, and with the same caution they emerged through some brambles into what appeared to be the ruins of a cottage. How appropriate, Hanny thought, to go out of a ruined house at one end, into a ruined house at the other end, with about eight hundred years between the two.

Even though it was now dark, Mr Bacon was very cautious as he stepped out of the ruined house into a short lane. He hurried along it, looking this way and that until he reached a small bridge over a stream. On the other side, he took out a large key and opened a wooden door. Hanny was briefly back in darkness, but a candle was lit, and he followed his leader into a small kitchen, in which candles were already burning. Mr Bacon pointed to a wooden table, and they both sat down, opposite each other.

And they looked at each other.

Hanny could feel his own frustration burning in the great man. If only Mr Bacon were French, or even German, there would be some words with which they could communicate. Or Latin. That might help. But he'd never learned it, never been taught it, never been interested in it. He'd heard of 'Amo, amas, amat, but it was no good telling this bearded old man that he loved him. The same applied to 'Veni, vidi, vici.' How about came, saw, was captured?

He vaguely remembered a teacher saying that Latin was the

basis of French and Italian, from which English had taken and adapted many words. But which words, and in which form?

He decided to make a start with the name of their enemy. "Vadigan," he said slowly and precisely, then scowled and made a thumbs-down gesture.

The scientist understood. He made a whooshing sound and made a rapid right to left movement with his arm, and pointed to Hanny

Yes, nodded Hanny. He made his own whooshing sound, swept his arm across from left to right, and did a theatrical shrug, finishing with a sad look.

Again, Mr Bacon understood.

"Book."

It sounded like a blend of 'bawk', 'bok' and 'boke', but it was clear enough.

"Yes," Hanny replied, then changed it to "Yea."

He decided that it was time for pantomime. He held up a finger to indicate the number one. He said, "Vadigan," crossed two fingers and formed his hands into the prayer position; then pointed at himself and did another whoosh. Next, two fingers, to indicate the number two. He gestured tearing a book to shreds.

Mr Bacon said something which sounded like 'there?' Did he mean 'Where? Where is the sphere?' Was that what he meant?

With signs, sounds and pantomime, Hanny tried to convey that the sphere was in a field, on the other side of the swamp.

The scientist slowly stood and paced about the kitchen. Abruptly, he stopped and looked at Hanny, as though he had seen him for the first time. He walked quickly to a cupboard, opened it and pulled things out. Moments later, he brought a wooden plate of bread and cheese, and a glass of wine. Hanny said, "Thank you," with deep feeling. Time travel problems and Vadigan problems were pushed aside while he tucked in to the best meal he'd ever had. And he didn't hesitate to drink the wine. He deserved it.

When Hanny started to eat, Mr Bacon went out through an internal door. He looked in a couple of times, which made Hanny think he was in a hurry. He tried to eat quickly, but the food was too delicious to be rushed. And when he did finish, he wasn't in a hurry to do anything. What he would have liked to do was explore this place and time at his leisure with his wise guide and protector beside him. Imagine it! A living history lesson. When a history teacher said a wrong thing, Hanny could say, "Actually …", and tell the teacher and the class what really happened, and what things, and people, were really like.

What a wonderful way to learn, and teach, history!

He became aware that Mr Bacon was quietly inviting him to follow, through the same door by which they had entered. Oh, well, so now back to being furtive and nervous, and scuttling around, like a couple of mice when the owl is about. Realising that he had neither the words nor the understanding for a discussion, he decided to continue doing as he was told.

And furtive it was. It soon became clear that they were returning to the cave. But why? Was he to be hidden there? For how long?

The old woman was expecting them. She was wearing a long shawl, and she held a long staff. Mr Bacon gestured and said, "Edith."

Hanny pointed at himself and said, "Hanny."

Much nodding indicated unanimous satisfaction.

Hanny was surprised when they went out of the front of the cave. Mr Bacon indicated to Hanny that he should hold his cloak, as he had done before. Seeing what they were about to do, Hanny was very willing to do as advised.

They were going to walk across the swamp.

Edith led the way, slowly, seeming to know where she was

going, but testing the ground at each step with her staff. Hanny
was apprehensive, but pleased that they were heading for the
sphere. If he couldn't look round here in peace, then he wanted
to be home again.

Slowly, they made their way over the soggy ground. A mist
had risen, or descended, and from over to their right came only
an occasional muffled sound of a cart wheel or a voice. One big
difference, Hanny thought, between our time and theirs was that
in this time, you could be utterly, silently alone. And almost
blind, in the absence of house lights, street lights, vehicle lights.

He instantly revised his assessment when a figure appeared,
seeming to rise out of the ground, and called to them.

Vadigan.

He was holding the book aloft with one hand, and he
seemed to be accusing Hanny's companions of being witches.
That's what it sounded like. Then he spoke to Hanny.

"Hanny! You let me down. You let your sister down. I
promised to protect you."

"By making me sleep on a stone bed, by making me work all
day, with nothing but a bowl of the worst porridge I've tasted?"

"All that is good for you, Hanny, for your character, for your
soul."

"These two people have taught me more about goodness
than you've ever done. And their food's much better. You need to
improve your own character. You stole Mr Bacon's book, and
you stole me."

"Let's test Mr Bacon, shall we? I'm going to offer an
exchange. You for the book."

"But you said you're going to destroy the book. Why would
he choose the book?"

"He would have it long enough to hide it, make copies
of it."

He called to Mr Bacon. Hanny recognised 'boy' and 'book',

and knew the rest. He looked anxiously at his protector. The opportunities to make the most of his possession of the book must have occurred to him, too.

Mr Bacon's response was immediate. He spoke quickly to Edith, took her staff, and walked quickly towards Vadigan. Edith took a few steps forward, calling. She was ignored. Vadigan stared at the man who walked rapidly towards him, ignoring the dangerous ground. He cried out and stepped aside. In the same moment, both men sank to their knees. Edith and Hanny rushed forward to grab their leader. Vadigan lurched, staggered and floundered into the deepest part of the swamp. He shouted, pleaded and prayed. But there was no safe way of going to help the sinking man.

Vadigan and the book sank quickly out of sight.

He had done what he wanted to do.

His failure was his victory.

He had destroyed the book.

CHAPTER TWENTY-FOUR

They waited for a long time, watching the place in the swamp where Vadigan, and the book, had disappeared. Eventually, with a sigh, Mr Bacon put his hands on the shoulders of his companions and they left the sad scene. No longer in danger from Vadigan, they retraced their steps to Edith's cave. When Mr Bacon intimated by gestures that they would go to the sphere by a much less dangerous route, Hanny plunged into excited pantomime, explaining that he wanted to have a short guided tour before he left.

That was clearly approved. With a last affectionate parting from the old woman, Hanny was taken back to the kitchen, where, to his great pleasure, he was given a duplicate of his earlier meal. After that, he was given a straw mattress and left to sleep in the warm kitchen.

For a few seconds, Hanny wondered whether it was inconsiderate of him to want to delay his return when his sister, and her friend, must be very anxious about him. And that was assuming that the sphere was still there, intact, and functioning perfectly. One good thing about the menace of Vadigan was that he had kept Hanny's mind off such worries as his attempt to return.

Just before the released worries rushed in, he fell asleep.

* * *

It was barely light when Hanny was roused from a deliciously deep sleep. Breakfast was porridge, much better than the monks' version, but still not something that he enjoyed. He wasn't being fussy. He didn't want anything fancy. Just some bread and cheese would have been fine for him. But he smiled at his benefactor, and looked suitably satisfied. When he was given a glass of ale to drink, he decided that he'd make the tour a short one, and hurry home before he turned into a drunkard.

It *was* a short tour. Hanny was enjoying walking though the busy main street, appreciating the noise and smells as a tourist would, noticing every cart having its own separate noise instead of a merged din, fascinated by the raucous shouting, the cows, dogs and pigs wandering about, the heaps of dung, the strange and intense smells, the timber-framed houses. People were so busy, few were not active. They huffed and grunted and heaved, and wagons and carts rumbled and rattled along, some pulled by horses, some by people. Even children were working. It was wonderful to see, from the inside as it were, even being touched by passing people.

But he wasn't surprised when it came to a sudden end. Alerted by Mr Bacon's sudden exclamation, he looked ahead. Three monks, accompanied by some official-looking men, were walking towards them.

Hanny was spun round and pulled along by the surprisingly alert and dextrous scientist. They ducked into an alley, through a small door, and into a room filled with sacks of flour. They went across and through another door, into another alley.

Through his fear and excitement, Hanny was indignant, for himself and for Mr Bacon. What way was this to treat a great scientist? And what way was this to treat a tourist?

They dodged and ducked and wove in a complicated route through the town, suddenly emerging onto the firm ground beside the swamp. Prompted by his companion, Hanny pointed.

Moments later, he was relieved to see it still there, and to stand in front of it. Mr Bacon pointed at Hanny, then mimed the breaking of things. Hanny understood. And he understood that no goodbye outside death had ever had such finality. He felt a sorrow that he'd never felt before. He could see the sadness in Mr Bacon.

They heard angry shouts. The little crowd of pursuers was advancing. Mr Bacon muttered and shook his head. Abruptly, as though he couldn't bear any more, he picked Hanny up and threw him into the sphere.

CHAPTER TWENTY-FIVE

"...IDEA," EDIE WAS SAYING, WHEN HANNY FLEW OUT OF the sphere and collided with her. She didn't mind the pain. The double joy of having her brother back, in almost the same moment in which he'd left, and of not having to explain to their parents about his absence, put her in the best mood of her life.

For a nervous moment, she looked at the sphere, half-expecting the arrival of Vadigan. Hanny saw her looking and said, "It's all okay, Edie. No more Vadigan."

She was eager to hear all about it, but Nico pointed out that it was late, and they'd been away from home for a long time. So, the full explanation was deferred until the next day.

"I'll be patient," Nico said, "but I expect you'll be going through it tonight."

Hanny winked. "I'll make it just as exciting for you, Nico."

Edie and Nico started to move away, but Hanny said. "You're forgetting. " He waved a hand at the sphere. "I've been told what to do by Mr Bacon."

He picked up a large piece of plaster, and hit the glass jars and tubes. The sphere disappeared.

"Oh," Edie said. "So, it's finished."

"Yes."

Then Edie said, "Just a moment. *Mr Bacon*? You met Mr Bacon?"

Hanny grinned and said, "I did more than meet him. I was with him in his house, and in an old woman's cave, and in the swamp where Vadigan died. And before that, I was imprisoned in a monastery, and escaped by climbing over a wall."

Nico said, "Right. We can go through it again tomorrow, but we can talk as we walk, and you can give us the short version."

It seemed odd to walk though the scene of so much drama. They all felt it and thought it as they crunched through the broken glass and masonry. When they reached the hall, Nico turned and said wistfully, "So much, all to be kept secret, because no-one would believe."

Edie added, "It's already not in Mr Bacon's history, and it won't be in ours."

"Or anyone's," Hanny said, not wanting to be left out, but making the most upsetting comment of all.

"Well ... come on," Nico said. "No point in moping about it. Home, and let's have some information as we go."

They walked through the front door and stopped. Three policemen were standing at the gate, looking at them in a puzzled and scrutinising way.

"What were you kids doing in there? Don't you know its dangerous? Didn't you read the signs? Or did you think you knew better?"

Edie said quietly, "Ah, the every popular multiple questions." She called, "We were just looking. We were very careful. Yes, we know it's dangerous, we read the signs, and we were reckless."

"What were you doing in there?" The question was asked with heavy suspicion.

Nico said, "We weren't doing anything wrong. We were just curious. It was a challenge because it's dangerous and said to be haunted."

"Those aren't good reasons."

"No. We're young and reckless."

"Young and stupid, more like. Anyway, we're here on more important business. Did you see anyone else in there?"

"A man was there earlier, but he left some time ago."

"What sort of man? What did he look like?"

"Tall and thin, nicely dressed, very irritable about something. He seemed to be conducting some experiments, glass jars and a bunsen burner, which made me think he might be the person who stole laboratory equipment from our school."

"In what way was he irritable?"

"We were interfering with his experiment."

Hanny called, "He said if his experiment failed, he was going to smash his equipment and give up."

Edie had been keeping roughly to the truth, but Hanny had told a straight lie. But he had anticipated that the police would go inside to look for clues and corroborative evidence, and they would see the broken equipment. In an instant, he had realised this, decided, and delivered a necessary lie.

Was there such a thing in the great code of ethics?

"Did he bother you at all? Threaten you?"

"Difficult to say," replied Nico, which it was unless he was to add another lie. "He certainly did a lot of angry muttering. We went off, and when we returned, he disappeared. The jars and bottles were all smashed."

Edie almost smiled. Nico had stated facts, not the exact sequence. So not even a necessary lie.

"Is he dangerous?" Edie asked.

"He could be. You children should heed warnings and stay

well away from a place like this, and if you see the man again, let us know immediately."

"Yes, sir."

They walked quickly away, exhausted by the mental manoeuvring. Hanny tried a very brief summary of his visit to thirteenth century Oxford, but that just made the others more eager for information. By the time that they parted, he had filled in some blanks, but held back sufficient information to be sure of a rapt audience the next day.

As he and Edie continued on their way, he said, "It wouldn't be fair on Nico to tell you everything now."

"No, I suppose not. On the other hand, I could apply the torture when you're in bed."

They laughed together. That was nice.

They were still smiling when they walked into their kitchen.

Their parents weren't smiling.

"Where have you been?"

"Do you know what the time is?"

"We've been worried sick."

Edie and Hanny looked at each other, as they floated down from their euphoric cloud.

"Sorry," Edie said. "We lost track of the time."

Hanny said, "It was a good game, and I just became ... carried away."

Good answers, they both thought. Almost through the danger.

"Hanny."

"Yes, mum?"

"Where are your clothes?"

"Ah," Hanny said. "Now, *that's* a very good question.

CHAPTER TWENTY-SIX

"I was impressed," Edie said to Nico.

"I learnt from the best," Hanny said with a modest smile.

They were sitting on a log in the garden of the ruined house. With its reputations for danger and being haunted, it was a good place in which to escape from the crowds.

Edie added, "And none of it was a lie. He *did* fall, he *was* rescued, he *was* given some clean clothes. Just not quite as he described it."

"A necessary bending of the truth," said Nico,

"Exactly."

"Appropriate for my little theory about what happened."

"Tell me again."

"Right. Now, it's not the same thing, this is just for illustration. You are on a train going from Oxford to London. At some point on your journey, you will meet and pass a train going from London to Oxford. The reverse journey. Or, for some people, the return journey. Or, the second part of the same journey. If you go to London and come back to Oxford, it could be said that your journey is from Oxford to Oxford, going this way, then that way. Now, if time didn't just go in a perpetual straight line, but curved around, it might be possible to look across, as with the train travellers, and see people on a different part of the same journey."

"So, instead of looking through time, Mr Bacon and I looked across at each other?"

"Yes. That's it. Call it a working theory."

Hanny joined in. "It's as good as anything."

"Thank you, Hanny. Yes, it's better than no theory at all. But we can never support the theory with our experience because our experience can't be used."

Edie said, "What about the distance from Folly Bridge to my house?"

"Yes, that is a tricky one. My suggestion is that the upper parts of the Earth's surface are constantly sliding around; over eight hundred years, perhaps there was some stretching."

"But Folly Bridge hasn't moved."

"In relation to the rest of Central Oxford, which might have moved, too."

He saw the doubt in Edie's eyes. "Okay. It's weak. That leaves the alternative."

"Which is?"

"That the time link came to you because … well, because you have a special quality. Or quali*ties*.

"Oh, really."

Nico winked at Hanny. "I knew that explanation would embarrass her."

Edie quickly said, "We've all agreed that this must be a secret, but do you think we should write it down, for posterity, for curious people who might come long after we're dead?"

"Yes, I do. And not just because it was something wonderful that happened. Vadigan's defeated and dead, hundreds of years ago, when everything was very different. But in one way, things weren't different at all. There is always someone who says that the truth has been revealed, in a book, or by a person, and what was written or said must be believed; there's no need to think about it; in fact, thinking about it is wrong. And thinking about it goes from wrong to illegal to forbidden. Don't think! Believe what you're told to believe! There are always the Vadigans opposing the Roger Bacons. I've read about Bruno, burned at the stake for thinking and saying things which weren't approved by the Catholic Church."

"By the time anyone reads our book, it might be too late."

"Well, then, we'll do it now, for people to read now. But we'll do it as a story, just a product of our imaginations, with our little warning. People prefer stories anyway, not accounts of things which really happened."

"Oh, what shall we call it?" Hanny asked.

"You choose, Nico," Edie said.

"I suggest The Man from Folly Bridge. All agreed?"

"Yes," Edie and Hanny said together.

And that is what they did.

THE END

ACKNOWLEDGMENTS

As always, to Robert Harrison at Seneca Author Services for his continued help and support.

ABOUT THE AUTHOR

John Guthrie writes speculative fiction for all ages, from children to adults. His books are often set in troubled worlds, whether here on earth or in far-flung planets in other solar systems. At the heart of his books are characters happy with their quiet lives who are ensnared in situations they're desperate to escape from. They don't know whom to trust because trusting the wrong person often leads to the worst possible outcome. You'll find yourself cheering for each of the main characters in John's books as they match wits with the most ruthless of adversaries.

John resides in the UK and, when he's not on the lookout for a stray dog to show up on his doorstep, is continually dreaming up new stories and characters.

If you enjoyed this story, please consider leaving a review at your favorite book site.

Follow John on Facebook at tinyurl.com/5n82ch69, and for a full list of his books, visit www.john-guthrie-author.com.